# bright
## coin
## moon

# bright
# coin
# moon

**KIRSTEN LOPRESTI**

Sky Pony Press
New York

Sky Pony Press books may be purchased in bulk at special discounts for sales promotion, corporate gifts, fund-raising, or educational purposes. Special editions can also be created to specifications. For details, contact the Special Sales Department, Sky Pony Press, 307 West 36th Street, 11th Floor, New York, NY 10018 or info@skyhorsepublishing.com.

Sky Pony® and Sky Pony Press® are registered trademarks of Skyhorse Publishing, Inc.®, a Delaware corporation.

Visit our website at www.skyponypress.com.

10 9 8 7 6 5 4 3 2 1

Library of Congress Cataloging-in-Publication Data is available on file.

Cover design by Erin Seaward-Hiatte

Print ISBN: 978-1-62914-751-2
Ebook ISBN: 978-1-63220-204-8

Printed in the United States of America

*To Tony, Julia, and Natalie*

# bright
## coin
# moon

# ONE

I slid open the screen door and stepped into the night. A pale, pockmarked moon hovered in the branches of a cedar tree. I took out my Moon Sign notebook and wrote:

*Full moon on a Moon Day (Monday). It means good luck, unless you view it through tree branches, which I did. Then it becomes a ruined moon. Is ruined luck bad luck or is it no luck at all?*

I heard footsteps on the path and turned. My mother was walking up in her Sizzler Steak House apron and her squeaky restaurant sneakers.

"That you, Lindsey?" she asked.

"Who else would it be?"

She stepped into a puddle of porch light and stopped. Her blond hair was up, clipped at the top in a way that exaggerated her round face, and she was wearing the pink frosted lipstick she always wore to work—the same color she wore the day she won the Miss Oregon Pageant almost twenty years ago. Kissably Pink, that's what Revlon used to call the shade. She had to order it mixed now because they'd discontinued it.

She walked over to the trashcan, pulled off her Sizzler Steak House apron, and threw it in.

"Good night at the Steak House?" I asked.

"I was fired."

"You were fired?" I repeated. It didn't completely surprise me. She was always losing jobs. Still, it was alarming. We had a stack of bills on our kitchen table—first, second, and third notices.

"They accused me of stealing money from the register. Can you believe it?"

I could. She'd done this before. "Did you?"

"Did I what?"

"Steal money from the register."

"*Stealing* is such a harsh term. I wouldn't call it stealing exactly."

I sighed. The stealing itself didn't bother me as much as the fact that she hadn't been careful about it. Why couldn't she be careful once in a while?

"Well, do you have the money at least?"

If she had it, the situation wasn't completely hopeless. We could at least pay some of our bills.

"No." She sat down on the porch step and rested her head on her knees. She looked so sad, slumped like that; I couldn't help but feel sorry for her.

"Well, it's done," I said. "How about we watch the Miss Oregon videos and forget about it?"

It always cheered her up to watch those videos. We had one of the Miss America pageant, too, but we never watched that one. That one she lost.

"Not tonight," she said. "Just go open the shop. I'll be there in a second."

Our shop—the psychic reading business we ran out of our garage. We'd been at it since I was seven—ten years

2

now. She'd been at it longer, her whole life. Her mother had trained her and then she had trained me. I don't know whose mother trained whom before that, but my mother claimed our ancestors were traveling gypsies who could look into the future and understand people's dreams. I had the dark eyes, she said, and the long straight brown hair to prove it. It could be true. Half of what my mother said at any given time generally was, but if so, by the time the magic got down to us, it was diluted. My mother and I didn't have one drop of psychic ability between us.

I wasn't in any great hurry to open up the shop, but I said, "Sure. Someone might come."

We both laughed at how hollow my voice sounded; then she stood up and started for the garage. I followed. We passed a rose bush, some chipped angel statues, her hubcap-turned-birdbath, and her hanging kitchen spoon/wind chime collection, then we ducked under a trellis and came up under our neon psychic reading sign. The sign hadn't worked since the morning my mother hit it for the third time with her car, but in a great show of optimism, I turned it on. It flashed for a second and went off, a brief green buzz in the night.

She rolled up the door and we stepped inside. I sat down at the card table, on a purple star-spangled cushion, and she walked over to the counter, to the part of our garage where other people might park a car.

"Did you eat?" She opened the lid of the Crock-Pot she kept out there and, like a detective, announced, "You didn't." She carried the Crock-Pot over and set it down in front of me. A gulp of brown liquid sloshed out.

I leaned forward and peered in. I didn't have high expectations. My mother liked to cook, but she didn't

3

like to follow recipes. She never seemed to have the right ingredients on hand, so she used what she had, and she didn't own a measuring cup. She just didn't see cooking as the precise science it is. Her bread didn't rise, and her cakes fell flat. Her sauce was as watery as tomato soup. Most of the time, she just threw whatever she had in her Crock-Pot, turned it on low, and let it stew for several hours.

She dropped a lumpy pile on both our plates then reached beneath the table for her small, battery-operated television.

"Let's find a movie," she said.

"Nah," I said. I didn't like watching movies with her. She talked too much. She didn't pay attention or let you pay attention, unless a sad ending came up, in which case she'd start bawling as though she'd watched the whole thing. I set my fork down and looked out the open door. It was raining. Water swirled down the driveway and out to the gravel road.

"Well, *Dateline*, then," she said. "It should be good tonight. They're going to expose Hollywood psychics."

That sounded okay to me, so I agreed.

She reached for the remote, and we squinted at the fuzzy screen. The show began with a shot of the Hollywood sign.

"Hollywood," a voice-over said, "has long been home to some of the most famous psychics of our time, the so-called psychics to the stars. But who are these psychics? And are they for real?"

A reporter appeared on the screen. "Tonight," he said, "we will go behind the scenes to catch phony Hollywood psychics in the act." The camera moved to the side, and a man in shorts and a Hollywood T-shirt appeared. Instead of a microphone, he held a backpack, and he had a camera with a long strap around his neck. He was supposed to look like a tourist, he told us, pointing at his shirt.

"He's cute," my mother said. She waved her finger to scold him. "Cute, but tricky."

"Do you think he could trick us?" I asked.

"Sure," she said. "He looks like anyone else."

I looked back at the screen. The reporter walked into a Los Angeles fortune parlor through a curtain of beads, and a woman in hoop earrings greeted him. She didn't read the tarot or ask for his palm or even say very much, but she spoke in a soft, pleasant voice and what she said made sense in a general way. It might have been a good reading, overall, if she hadn't told the reporter who walked in next the exact same thing. The word EXPOSED popped up in bold white letters across the fortune-teller's face.

"That woman is stupid," I said.

"She has no imagination," my mother agreed. "She deserves what she gets."

The *Dateline* crew then visited the office of Madame Zoya. She was the most famous of all the Hollywood psychics, a voice-over said, but they couldn't get in to see her. Her secretary, a woman with neon green hair, put them on an eight-month waiting list.

The crew didn't have time to wait. They had a segment to film, after all. After a short commercial break, they came back with a shot of Madame Zoya poolside, outside her Malibu mansion. She pulled her long hair up and fastened it at the base of her neck with a rubber band, then she turned over and continued to sun herself.

The show broke for a commercial, but I kept thinking about Madame Zoya. I liked the limo she rode in and the huge, Spanish-style house that she retreated into at the end of the show.

My mother waved a burnt potato in the air. "Did you see her house?"

"I saw it."

"And her limo! Now, that was nice. She gets to hang out with all those movie stars, like she's a celebrity herself. It's not fair." She turned the television off and leaned back in her chair. "You know what? We should move to California."

It seemed unfair to me, too. Those psychics were doing the same thing we were for more money, but it didn't mean I wanted to go to California.

"We're not moving to California."

"What do we have here? Name one thing."

"I have school. Friends. You have your job." I stopped because that wasn't right. Also, I'd thought of something. If she was thinking of going, she must have some money. "You still have it don't you? How much did you steal tonight?"

"Pocket change. Not enough to get going."

"Well, that settles it then."

"You know," she said, "I don't understand you. I thought you'd be all for it. You're always talking about that California school, how much you want to go next year. I say, let's go early. Let's get to California, get started."

It was true. I wanted to go to UC Santa Cruz. They had one of the top five astronomy programs in the country and a tremendous observatory, but it wasn't true that it was something I talked about much. I never talked about it, actually. I had my grades up pretty high, but I guess I was afraid that talking about it might jinx it. It irritated me that she was talking about it.

"California is *my* thing," I snapped.

"You own California? Because the last time I checked . . ."

She stopped. A shadowy, slightly bent person was walking up the path. He stepped around the wishing well and through our entrance awning of flowers. Barney Wilcox, our least favorite client. He visited too often. He complained about everything, and he didn't always pay.

"Not it," my mother and I said at the same time.

"It's you," I said. "It's so you."

She frowned. She could be a sore loser sometimes. She pushed at the garage remote frantically, trying to shut the door, but it wouldn't budge. After a second or two, I pried the remote out of her hand.

"Don't try to get out of it," I told her. The way I saw it, she didn't have much choice. He might pay. She'd lost her job. We needed the money.

"We're closed," she called out in a singsong voice.

"Closed, you say?" Mr. Wilcox was in the doorway now. He held his cane in the air like a conductor and poked our OPEN FOR BUSINESS sign. A rusty, metal note rose up beside him in the dark yard. "The sign here says different."

"Well, you can't trust signs," my mother said.

Mr. Wilcox scratched his head. He must not have known for sure whether a person could trust signs. He looked down at his giant black-and-orange sneakers as if he were, just now, noticing them for the first time. In his day, Mr. Wilcox owned a shoe business, a place called Longfoot Shoes. Shoes for the tall and the small and the

7

hard to fit, half and quarter sizes, and five different widths. Longfoot Shoes provided an expensive, though not particularly stylish, product to a tiny, almost non-existent market, but for a time it was successful.

The sale of the shoe business left Barney Wilcox with more than enough money (a small fortune some people said), but when his dog got sick last year, he refused to pay for a vet. He'd had that cocker spaniel for ten years. It never left his side, but that was the kind of friend he was to it in the end.

A psychic reader should never pass judgment on clients. That's what my mother says. Like them too much, and you can't fool them. Dislike them too much, and you can't see into their hearts. But sometimes, I'd look at Barney Wilcox and think *dog killer*. I couldn't help it. He was a dog killer. How could he ever be anything else?

"Why don't you hustle on off to that steak house or wherever you're going, Debbie. Lindsey will take care of me."

My mother smiled. She looked slightly hurt, but also victorious. "You heard the man, Lindsey. He wants you." She stuffed her tarot cards into her purple speckled sack and shuffled off toward the house.

"I'll do your tea leaves," I told him, "but that's all." If he paid, I could always read his cards, but I wasn't going to promise it, right off.

Barney Wilcox stepped into the garage and shook the rain out of his hat. It was a strange, checkered flat cap hat, but his hair, underneath it, was much worse. It twirled in one long silver piece around the top of his head like the tail of a rat. Rain clung to his eyebrows and sloshed in his shoes.

I set a cup of hot tea in front of him, and he stared at it suspiciously. Every now and then when I read for him, he'd get this wild idea I'd poisoned him. He'd stand up suddenly, knock the table over, and shout, "There's something squirrelly in my drink. Something squirrelly!"

"Drink it," I told him, "swirl it three times clockwise, turn it over and back."

He did as I said, then he set the cup on the table and looked inside.

"It's bad," he said, "oh, it's bad." But this didn't surprise or frighten him as much as you might think.

"Let me look." I stared down at the shapes the leaves made and tried to puzzle something, anything out. It was a bit like finding cloud shapes in the sky. In the end, as always, any answer seemed to fit, so I told him I saw a rainbow of peace and good luck.

"What's that you say? A rainbow?" Clearly, he didn't believe a word of it. I tried to tell him that I saw the sun, but he saw the rain. My flower was his umbrella and my present was his coffin.

"Tell it to me straight," he kept saying. "The truth this time, what do you see?"

I was starting to get frustrated. I didn't want to tell a bad fortune, and I didn't know why he had to demand it. "I do see one small bad thing," I said, finally, to appease him. "The rest of your hair is going to fall out."

He gripped the ten or fifteen strings of hair on his head, and his mouth flew open. His eyebrows went up into two V's. "It's just hair," he said, "but just the same, I'd like to keep it."

We both sat in silence for a few seconds absorbing the bad news about his hair, until he said, "Ah, it's all hogwash."

I nodded. I agreed. What could I say to that?

He coughed twice. Then he raised his eyebrows in a naughty way and asked for a love potion.

"Fifteen dollars," I said. "Plus you owe ten for the last one."

He launched into his various, familiar explanations as to why he couldn't pay. His tea was too cold. His cup was chipped. In the shoe business, they knew how to please a customer. If they couldn't fit your foot, they'd give you a set of socks for free.

I opened my mouth to argue with him, but then I realized the uselessness of it. He wasn't going to pay.

"Ever heard of something called a money tree?" I asked.

He leaned forward. I guess the word *money* caught his attention. "Tree, you say?"

The idea of the money tree comes from an old gypsy scam. The way it works is this: you pretend to own a tree in your yard that multiplies buried money. You tell the client to bury their money. Then you dig it up. It sounds very simple. I know. Most of the old tricks do. But if you can find the right mix of greedy, yet gullible person, it's surprisingly effective.

Mr. Wilcox tapped his hearing aid in an interested way. "You bury money, you say?"

I nodded. "Just my fees. Then, when it doubles, you give me half."

He looked surprised, like he might have thought half was too much, so I added, "Readings aren't free. It's a business."

I looked up at the glow-in-the-dark stars on the garage ceiling and thought about just how much I disliked the psychic reading business. It wasn't the lying, I decided, or not completely. It wasn't even the waiting. It was more that it seemed to me, if I continued to sit in the garage each night, I might only have a very short amount of time left before some type of terrible transformation took place. I would solidify, spread out. Sprout bunions on my toes. I'd grow blond hair and a Sizzler Steak House apron and hum when it rained and forget about the dishes and spread restaurant crackers on the windowsills to feed the birds. At one point, my mother, too, had wanted to do something else. I looked out at the dark lawn, at the wind-filled trees, and for a second the whole yard seemed to waver, to draw in too close.

Mr. Wilcox nodded in a sly way, stood and shuffled out the door. When he came to the place where his path crossed the money tree, he stopped and thumped it with his cane. He circled the lawn a few times, as if he were thinking it over, then he zigzagged back to it like a crow to a shiny piece of paper.

After he left, I rolled down the garage door and walked out to the yard. The rain had stopped, but the air still smelled of it—the scent of an old wet shoe. I sat down on a tree stump and watched my mother move through the lit rooms of the house. It was just a small, brown box, but it was ours, and we'd lived there as long as I could remember. The shotgun house. That's what we called it, what everyone did, because of the way the front door lined up perfectly with the back. If you shot a bullet through one door, it would come out the other, or that's the theory. It was an odd house anyway, full of strange sounds and uneven corners and tight, cramped spaces. Living in the shotgun house was, I suppose, a bit like living in a pipe or a tunnel, but it had its good points. It had a nice, wide porch with a porchswing and a handful of blue metal chairs that sat in a row, facing the yard and the sunken steps. Leaves collected on this porch and birds landed, and sunny puddles popped up and filled with tadpoles. Acorns rolled across it during the day and smacked at the door at night, and small, hard, green apples made moon-shaped dents in the wood. The house was warm in the winter, cool in the summer, and in the spring the wind passed through it like one long breath. In the fall, it softened and sunk, bees buzzed around it, and leaves poked out from its roof tiles like feathers on a hat. I loved the shotgun house in the fierce, puzzling way you can come to love old battered things, but my mother always said the best thing about it was that as soon as you entered it, you were already leaving it. In a way, I suppose, both of us were right. It was an ugly house, but not a bad one. Still, we were ashamed of it. The whole time we had lived in it, we had wanted something better.

Somewhere in the distance, a coyote barked. A low, solitary moan, followed by the yip yap noise that proclaimed a kill, and I imagined him dancing. I pictured him with a fiddle, like the coyote characters that populated the stories my mother used to tell me, two-stepping in boots and a hat, dancing his thieves' dance under the light of the same, pale moon.

# TWO

I went to check the money tree the next morning, but my mother stopped me at the door.

"Are you wearing the same thing you wore yesterday?" she asked.

She must have thought that because my clothes looked the same, they were the same, but in actuality, I'd bought duplicates of the same outfit: ripped jean shorts and a black T-shirt. For a while last year, I tried to be fashionable, but then I decided that fashion, really, was about pleasing people, and what I'd rather do was displease my mother.

"I don't think so," I said.

"You could look so pretty, like one of those girls in the pageants, if you bothered to take the time."

Back in middle school, when I suddenly shot up taller than everyone else, she'd had the idea to put me in pageants, but then everyone else caught up height-wise. It turned out I wouldn't be tall after all, so she dropped the idea, which was fine with me. Being a psychic reader in a small town felt enough like being on a stage.

She studied me some more. "Those are poor people clothes," she proclaimed.

"Excuse me," I said, brushing past her, "but I left my non-poor clothes in my private jet. If I can just get past you, I'll get them."

"Very funny," she said. She put her arm across the doorframe. "Where are you really going?"

"To check under the money tree," I said.

"Well, you can save your time and energy. I already went out there. He buried five dollars."

"That's it? Five dollars?"

"In change."

I sat down at the kitchen table and tried not to look at the stack of bills in the center. She'd crisscrossed them into a tower to make them look less threatening, but it hadn't worked. I picked up the cereal box to pour it, but nothing came out.

"You know," she said, "I've been thinking some more about that California thing."

"I'm not going to California," I said.

She nodded, and went back to eating her breakfast, but a week later, she brought it up again.

"I figured out how we can get the money together to go to California," she said.

We were out in the garage, playing a game of Go Fish with tarot cards and waiting for customers, but when she spoke, I laid my cards down.

"I'm not moving to California," I said. "I told you that."

"Well, you never know. You might change your mind."

I still didn't believe she was completely serious, but I was starting to suspect it enough to be irritated. "Do you think," I asked, "that if we moved out there, we could just read for movie stars? That no one's thought of that? Do you really think there are just all these openings available to read for movie stars?"

"You know what, Lindsey?" she said. "You're negative today. You've got a bad aura—really weak. You've got the kind of aura that sucks up everyone else's aura."

I laughed, then. The stupid way she talked about auras was one of the reasons we could never be psychics to the stars, why no one would ever take us seriously.

"You could try sometimes," she said. "Once in a while you could help me try to make things better for us."

She turned away from me and looked down, and I thought maybe I'd laughed too loud. What she had said was partly true. All my plans for next year—go to college, study astronomy, quit the psychic business—were all for me. Not for us. I hadn't stopped to think at all about what she might do.

I pushed the card table back and stood up.

"I need to get out for a while," I said.

"Suit yourself."

I left the garage and stepped out into the hot midday sun. My flip-flops made a hard, slapping noise as I walked down the stone path.

"Where are you going?" she called after me, but I didn't answer. I felt her eyes on me, hot as the sun, so I took big strides and thrust back my shoulders. I tried to look like I was headed somewhere great, somewhere she'd be just dying to know about but never would, but after I passed the yard, I realized that, really, I had nowhere to go. Our Oregon town was small, a real do-nothing place, and all of my friends were gone for the summer.

"Why don't you stay out for a while," she called out after me. "Don't come back right away. I could use some alone time."

Well, that was a lie if I'd ever heard one. She hated to be alone. If I tried to shut my bedroom door for fifteen minutes, she'd knock until I opened it. She was saying it so I'd do the opposite. It was only a piece of reverse psychology, but it hurt just the same.

I wandered out to the center of town, although there wasn't much there, just a few shops and a movie theater, a library behind that at the bottom of the hill. I walked through the hardware store for a while, and then a store that sold cards and glass figurines. The cross-eyed woman at the counter looked up from a magazine to watch me. I'd broken one of her figurines when I was four years old, and it had tarnished my reputation with her. There wasn't anything you could do in that town that didn't follow you around.

I left the store, and walked down to the river. I sat down on the grassy bank and watched water bugs walk along the surface of the water and thought about leaving home. It would be easy enough, I told myself. I only had to walk away. But I didn't really think I would do it. For one thing, I was seventeen and still in school. For another, I loved her. Even in my angriest moments, I did. I couldn't leave her without any money and all alone.

When I noticed the day had darkened, I scrambled up the bank to the empty road. This street wasn't ever crowded, but there was something about the emptiness on this particular evening that made me long to go home. The sky was almost black when I started back, and the street had turned blue. Insects stirred in the long grass beside my feet.

I was still a mile or two away when I smelled the smoke, but at first I didn't think anything of it. In the town where we lived, people often burned things: old papers, furniture, anything. It was a well-accepted alternative to visiting the dump or hiring a moving van, but something about the direction or the quantity of the smoke tonight seemed different. I pictured my mother on the couch, yawning, waking up from her long afternoon of alone time to a wall of flame and something in my chest froze. My knees trembled. I didn't think I could move, but suddenly I was running.

I stumbled into the yard, just as the fire trucks were pulling out. My mother was standing in the red streak of the taillights, a wild silhouette in a Big Bird bathrobe, backdropped by smoke and the ruined house.

"I thought you . . ." I said.

"Shh. I'm all right." The house made a dripping, popping sound behind us, but the yard was still. *It's over*, I thought. *She's safe.* I leaned against her and felt my entire body relax into her shoulder. Her shirt smelled like ash and sweat and a trace of something else. Gasoline.

"It'll be okay," she whispered. "I promise. And who knows, maybe we'll get some insurance money for the house. We'll go to California."

"California!" I stepped away from her, as though she had burned me, because, instantly, I knew. I understood. She did it. She was the one who set the fire.

"You set it!" I said.

The tone of my voice must have surprised her because she stepped back, too.

"It wasn't just your house," I shouted. "It was my house, too. Did you think about that?"

"Calm down, Lindsey. You're not thinking right."

She tried to touch my shoulder, but I shook her off. "*I'm* not thinking right?"

"It doesn't matter if I did it or not or why," she said, calmly. "We don't need it." In the dark, her eyes looked frightening. The flame of the fire was still in them.

"We don't need a house?"

She made her voice very soft. "Here," she said. She took something out of her bathrobe pocket, but I couldn't make it out in the dark. "I risked my life to save it from the flames. It's that thing you're always writing in."

My Moon Sign notebook. I threw it to the ground.

"I'm *not* going to California," I said.

"You'll go if I say so," she snapped.

I crossed my arms and glared at her in the dark. "I won't. Not now. Not ever with you!"

She walked off in the direction of the garage and I stood there, stunned, staring at the house. The wind blew, and a porch board toppled into the lawn. A pine tree waved a black branch in the wind like an angry arm. I had the sudden, terrible thought, watching it, that what I was looking at was not my own yard, but an alternate world: a surreal place of incredible risk and incalculable cost, where fire and trees and your own home meant nothing, and to want something and to take it were the very same thing.

I picked up my Moon Sign notebook and dusted off the soot. I tucked it under my arm and tried to act like I didn't care about it, but that night, in bed on a pull-out couch at a neighbor's house, I opened it and wrote:

*Chinless Moon. It clung to the horizon for a while, then vanished in black soot. Everything is gone. Burned. Lost.*

There wasn't much room on the page to write anything else. It was a book meant for gardeners; it had only enough space to write out what to plant, but it had a good moon table that listed the names of some of the moons my mother had taught me, as well as favorable and unfavorable days for the year I bought it. There were some good articles, too. One was on beauty; it explained when to file your fingernails if you wanted them to grow and which days to get your haircut. Others dealt with planting or when to destroy weeds and pests. My favorite one concerned the pull of the sky on arguments, warfare, and court cases. I'd shoved a good deal of folded paper into this section— different charts I'd drawn of various arguments I'd had with my mother and how they'd worked out. Each chart had a circle in the center, which I'd dissected into twelve pies and filled with astrology signs, planet angles, and a long list of positive and negative numbers. The first one said: *Gemini Rising. Aldebaran is conjunct the ascendant tonight. Mom's tactic: relentless complaining. My tactic: tuning her out. Verdict: Mom wins. Tonight we hang ugly, puke-colored curtains in the living room.*

I moved over to the window chair and picked up my pen. I put myself in the first house, the position of the elector, and I put my mother in the seventh, the position of the opponent. From there, I graphed all our recent arguments, starting with the one over who would read for Barney Wilcox—which she should not, it turned out, have won—and ending with the one tonight, when all planetary angles and astrological signs held solid against her until she disregarded all argument and did what she wanted.

*This is war*, I thought. *It's all-out war.*

19

The next morning, we returned home to survey the damage. The house wasn't as bad as I'd expected. It was still standing, anyway, but a thick layer of ash covered it both inside and out. The bottom floor, which consisted of the hall and kitchen and living room, still looked all right—wet, yet recognizable. But the second floor was another story. My mother's bedroom was the worst—a heap of black ash, and mine was not far behind. In the corner of what used to be my ceiling, a burning tree had left a hole, an opening like a door, and through this hole I could see birds and sky. If I had a ladder, I could climb into our house this way. The rain could, too, or the snow, or any type of animal or criminal. What had once been a safe place was now not, and I knew it would never be again. I would never again sleep comfortably in the shotgun house.

We climbed over the fallen fence and picked through the rubble in the yard, but we didn't find much: just a sooty shovel with a burnt black handle, a metal bucket, and the charred remains of a bag of mulch. These things were worse than useless and we hated them. None of them, anymore, were anything we would ever want.

"This is the work of a mentally ill person," I told my mother.

She looked surprised. I hadn't spoken to her since we stood on the street together the night before.

"It wasn't me," she said.

I considered the possibility that someone else might have set it. Customers, a lot of times, showed up in our yard yelling at us about this or that: a failed love potion, bad advice, or a candle that wouldn't light, but I didn't really think any of them would do *this*. Those types of things, generally, never escalated into something this extreme.

I looked past her, at the house, hunkered down like a charred shoebox at the top of the hill. The front door was open. The shutters gone. A piece of the roof hung off one side of it like a dangling ear. The stone path was still there, but streaked with gray, as if some ghost or wild spirit had lingered above it for a while before drifting off.

Well, I guess we should start packing up," she said. "Head out for California."

I shook my head.

"The house is gone, Lindsey. What do we have to lose?"

I had plenty to lose. I had good grades, one more year of school. The things I could still lose were piling up.

We cleaned the house as best we could. The bottom floor was easy. It still smelled like wet charcoal, but for the most part, it looked the same as it always had. It was livable, we decided, although only just barely. We moved back in and shouted at each other in the disinfected rooms.

At night, I had trouble sleeping. My mother slept too close to me on the pull-out couch, and she thrashed around and woke me. Sometimes I'd hear things.

Once a bat came in and I had to open a window to let it out. Its wing hit the sill before it looped out and mixed into the sky. I stood for a while, looking at the spot where it had just been. The night was blue outside, brighter than the room, and it seemed to stretch out in front of me. I felt helpless against it. It might never end.

I walked over to the steps and sat down on the bottom rung. The stairs to nowhere. That's what we called them now. I followed the runner to the top with my eyes and thought about walking up. I thought I might feel comforted to see my old room, even if the room wasn't there.

I grabbed a flashlight and started up the steps, swinging the beam along the wall. At the top, I stopped. I looked in the direction of my old room and tried to picture it as it was before the fire: the white bed, the bookshelf, the desk with the marker stains. It made me feel terrible to think about it, so I looked up at the hole in the roof instead.

Inside the hole, the sky was dark, a swirl of black dust. The tree leaves looked silver against it. For a second, I felt frightened. The sky looked ruined, a vast and fiery wasteland, and it seemed too close. I thought that, maybe, I could smell the stars burning.

# THREE

My mother decided we needed to change our names.

We were standing in the kitchen when she told me. We'd just finished eating dinner, and I was clearing the table. At first I thought it was a joke.

"Right," I said.

"I'm serious."

I looked at her again. She did look serious. "Why?"

"It's just a precaution. Everyone should have a fake ID. Don't you think?"

*She's playing a game with me*, I thought. *She's trying to make me believe she's in some kind of trouble in Oregon, so that I will agree to leave right now for California.*

She opened her laptop and motioned for me to come over.

"Hold on a second." I put down the plate I was rinsing and wiped the suds on a rag.

"Come on, already," she said, like it was this big hurry.

I sat down beside her at the table and waited. After a few minutes of searching, she pulled up a site called Documents for a New Life and pointed at a faceless man in a white cowboy hat on the screen.

"He's who they're all running from," she said.

I didn't think so. If she was right about him, then why was he wearing a white hat? Why was he the only human figure on a site that supposedly promoted hope and a new life? Still, I tried to be diplomatic. "I don't like him," I agreed. "There's something about him."

For the whole rest of the week, I thought about that cowboy. He'd jump into my mind at random, while I was doing the dishes or reading for a customer, and he'd gallop into my dreams to ask me for directions. He generally seemed bewildered when he popped up, not at all threatening. I never could figure out what it was about him that made me so nervous. Was it because he was lost or because he was hiding or simply because he was faceless? Which of these did I fear? Or were they, in the end, all the same thing?

I printed out his picture and pasted him into my Moon Sign notebook.

*What's really happening?* I wrote. *What is the truth?*

What if my mother really did do something major? She'd said she only stole pocket change from Sizzler, but what if it was more? What if she'd gotten in trouble for setting the fire? What if (and this was the one that terrified me) Barney Wilcox had buried a lot of money and she'd dug it up? I'd told him to bury the money. That one was my fault. And scams like that were hard to defend. People automatically assume *you* are the bad person if the elderly are involved. I imagined a knock at our door, my mother in handcuffs. She'd back away, fidget, irritate the police. She'd talk nonstop, try to explain her way out of it. My heart raced thinking about it. I might never get her back.

A few days later, my mother woke me in a panic. She pulled off my blanket and said, "The police are coming! Get in the car!"

I sat up and rubbed my eyes, but she was gone, already out the door. I found her standing in the driveway in her Big Bird bathrobe, loading the car with astonishing speed. She'd packed all our stuff in trash bags, and she was firing them off like bullets. One by one, they landed in the trunk or flew past it into the backseat. Some of them popped open. She didn't move to rearrange anything or put any- thing back in; she just heaved and threw. Her slippers made a scratching sound against the gravel drive.

"What's that sound?" she said when she saw me. "Did you hear a siren?"

I stopped, mid-step, to listen. I heard a bird chirp. I heard a rooster crow. I heard the wind rise up and roll an acorn across the front porch of the house, but I didn't hear a siren.

"I didn't hear it," I said. "You didn't either." But I wasn't completely sure. Maybe she had heard it.

"It's gone. It passed. Thank God. Now, Lindsey, I need you to trust me. I need you to get in the car."

Something about the too-quiet way she said it alarmed me. *The police are actually coming*, I thought. *She's done something. She could go to jail.*

"I don't want them to take you," I wailed.

"That's why we need to hurry."

I ran back into the house. I grabbed my notebook and a handful of clothes and ran out. On my way to the car, I bumped into my mother on the path.

"Watch out," she said. She disappeared into the house and returned with two more trash bags. I tried to help her load them, but she waved me away. The car shook when she shut the trunk.

"That's it," she said. "Nothing else will fit. Wait. What's that?"

"What?"

"On the ground over there? Is it a suitcase?"

I looked down at the lumpy brown garment bag behind me, a few inches from my feet. "I don't know what it is."

She stepped away from the car and picked up the bag. She struggled with the zipper for a second and then held up a pile of her dresses. "It figures," she said, but she tossed them behind her, hangers and all, onto the grass. They landed in a wild, mocking circle and, when the wind blew, they twisted in an angry way, like women thrown down. When we pulled out, they were still there.

The car thumped over a curb and onto the road, and I looked up at the sky. Last night's moon was still there, silver as a coin, just above the tops of the cedar trees that lined the side of the road.

"That's a Bright Coin Moon," I said.

"Doesn't matter," she said.

"What you leave behind today will rise up tomorrow."

She turned to look at me, and we veered dangerously close to the curb. "You know, for a phony psychic, Lindsey, you're awfully superstitious."

Maybe so, but we didn't make it to the next street before we literally left something behind. A twist-top trash bag popped out the back window and split open on the street.

"Our cake mixer," I said, straining my neck to see. "And one of our towels. Our TV remote." Our Crock-Pot rolled away like a wheel spun loose.

"We can't stop," my mother said.

I'd suspected as much. I turned around and tried not to look back. After a while, I even made a game out of it. I listened to our things fall and tried to guess what they were by the sound they made on the road. Was it our camera? Our dishes? The backpack I used to take to school? I told myself I didn't really care. I'd lost my friends, my home, my name, so what did I care about a dish or a backpack?

We drove most of the morning. In Eugene, we stole two boxes of hair dye from a Wal-Mart and then parked at a gas station to use the bathroom to dye our hair. We'd picked black for her and red for me, but in the end, I couldn't do it. My long brown hair was the one thing I liked about myself. I cried too much; it made her nervous and she couldn't mix it.

"I think you should just keep it the way it is," she said finally.

"But you'll get caught," I choked.

She put her hands on my shoulders. "Know what I think? Red is too stand-out, anyway. Blond is, too. It's different for me. I have the stand-out thing, already."

She threw the box meant for me in the trash, but she dumped her own black mix over her head without further comment. She paced back and forth for thirty minutes and then washed it out in the sink. The result, with her blue eyes and white, white skin, was Addams-family alarming. I wanted to cry again when I saw it—this time for her— but she didn't seem to care. She looked in the mirror, made a scary, scrunched-up face, and said, "I look like a Halloween person."

Her hair didn't bother her one bit, but the line-up of people, knocking on the restroom door, had made her angry.

"Go the hell away," she yelled through the door.

When we walked out, no one was there.

We climbed back into the car. I put my feet up on the dashboard and watched Oregon go by: fields and rocks, a slice of blue sea, and a stretch of tall cedar. I slumped down in my seat and put on my headphones. I turned the music up loud enough to drown out her voice, and we drove on. We passed a stump forest, with its long sad rows of chopped down trees, and a dozen or so worn out lumber towns, plain as thumbs, that dotted the coast.

After a while, I took out my Moon Sign notebook. I tapped the pencil eraser against the side of the book, thinking things out. The main problem, I decided, had to do with the psychic business itself, with the fact that it required two people to run it. One person (me) had to ask questions and spy and dig up information, so that the other person (her) could pretend to know it. It just wasn't something she could do by herself. I put my hand over the page so she couldn't see it and wrote:

1. *Move to California.*
2. *Establish Mom as a Hollywood psychic so that she can support herself.*
3. *Leave the psychic business!*
4. *Leave Mom!*

At the bottom of the page in big capital letters, I wrote: *FREEDOM.*

When we crossed the state line, my mother nudged me. "There it is," she said. "The famous WELCOME TO CALIFORNIA sign." I looked out the window, but we'd already passed it.

"It doesn't look any different than Oregon," I said. I'd expected to see palm trees when we crossed into California, but these trees were evergreen: a mix of pine and cedar, just like at home.

"That's because this is Northern California," she said. "Southern California will be different enough, wait and see."

We arrived in Santa Monica at 4:30 a.m.

"We're here!" my mother shouted.

I looked out the window at the pier.

"Look at that restaurant," I said. "The Lobster. A lobster would taste good."

"That, or McDonald's. Do you think there's a McDonald's around?"

I looked back at The Lobster. "How much do you think it would cost to eat at that place?"

"Too much. Anything more than McDonald's costs too much. Why do you think we always stop there?"

I must have looked disappointed because she said, "Put it on our list. When we have money, The Lobster is the first restaurant we'll go to."

*Put it on our list* was not just a figure of speech with us; we had an actual list. A sheet of pale green notebook paper that bore the title, "A List of Things for a Better Life." The first item on our list was a new house, the second a new car, the third horseback riding camp. We had some silly things after that, like trumpet lessons for my mother, and a couple sad things, one of which was sealant for my teeth. The dentist had told my mother that I had the kind of deep ridges in my molars that could turn into cavities at any time. He'd recommended sealant, but we'd decided not to pay for it and to take the risk. It always made me feel sad to see that item. Sometimes, when I read it, I could feel my teeth rotting.

We drove around lost for half an hour, while my mother pretended to know where we were. She turned the radio up and tapped out the beat of a song on the steering wheel.

"Let's just go to our hotel," I said.

"Hotel? Why would we do that when we have an apartment?"

"We have an apartment?" I asked.

She looked down at her map. "We do. I found it online. It's very nice. A prime piece of real estate. Good location. Lots of space. It has a pool. You'll love it."

"Maybe we should have looked at it first," I said.

"Maybe," she said. "You know what? I don't think we can go to our apartment right now, anyway. We can't just go to the rental office and expect to get in at four thirty. I'm not that tired. Are you? It's almost like I slept the night. Well, the night's gone anyway. Do you know what I want to do?"

"What?"

"I'd like to find the Hollywood sign and take our picture in front of it. That's what people always do at the end of a trip when they get to Hollywood. They take their picture in front of the sign. Keep an eye out for it, okay?"

"We're tired," I said to deter her. "And we don't look great." My mother liked to look good in pictures.

She tipped the car mirror toward her and moved her bangs around. "We look all right. Hey, there it is. I wonder how you get up there."

I saved the picture: mother and daughter in the early morning sun. She's moving. She'd set the camera, and there wasn't as much time as she thought. Her hair is a blur, her body liquid, her arms are flapping like a bird. I'm a little behind her, off to the side, and my head is turned. I'm looking at her instead of the camera. With my arms folded, my teeth clenched, and my brow curled, I look angry, shocked. I look half asleep. There is nothing in my posture that indicates what I was really feeling, what I remember thinking at that moment, just a few seconds after I had first glimpsed the sign and the vast, lit city below: This place is big. It's bright. It's loud, and we don't know anything about it. We have no idea how to live here.

# FOUR

The apartment complex was on South Sepulveda Boulevard, just below the 405. It was a squat, square, stucco structure with a wrap-around balcony, a slumped roof, and a bright, furious garden. Wind off the highway hit the face of the building in waves. It rattled the flowers and hurled tin cans at the windows before it rose up, swirling, to hover above the balcony in a black belt of dust. At night, through this film, the moon looked orange. It pulsed like a garden globe in the starless, Los Angeles sky.

"We can't live here," I said when I first saw it.

"We can't afford anything else."

My mother ducked inside to talk to the manager, and I walked around the building to the back to what, at one time, must have been a pool but was now just a concrete hole. When the wind blew, the tarp flapped up, and I could see what lay beneath: an inch or so of rain water, some cigarette butts, and a couple of beer cans bumping against each other like toy boats. I watched a fly touch down on the green water and studied the tadpoles that swam back and forth beneath the tarp.

*This is where we live now*, I thought. *This is our pool. The Sepulveda Apartment complex is Lindsey Smith's home.*

"Lindsey Smith," I said the name aloud. It sounded odd to me, and it felt strange on my tongue. I was used to Lindsey Allen, so it seemed too short. *Smith* came out too hard, like a punch at the end. If I said it over and over, I might get used to it. But I didn't really want to get used to it. I might become Lindsey Smith then, and I didn't want that. It had something to do with losing Lindsey Allen, of course, but there was more to it. The real Lindsey Smith was dead. Documents for a New Life had stolen her name, and I didn't know how she'd feel about that. My mother had said it was lucky that we could both keep our first names. But was it really lucky? I guess that depends on how you look at it. Certainly, it wasn't lucky for Lindsey Smith.

A yellow-billed seagull landed on the back of the plastic chair beside me.

"Hello," I said to it. It hopped from one foot to the other before it took off, its left wing slamming against the back of the chair.

I had no company now, not even the bird. I felt lonely suddenly, misplaced, as if I was waiting for someone to find me. It occurred to me that I needed some luck, so I dug a penny out of my pocket and threw it in the pool, but I didn't know what to wish for. Everything seemed so screwed up. The penny landed on the tarp and slid down into a puddle of dirty water.

"Wishing for me?" a voice asked. I turned to see a boy about my age with black hair, a square jaw, and broad shoulders. He had his arms crossed, and he stood slightly back, so that he appeared, almost, to rest against an invisible wall, just slightly behind and to the right of his shoulder.

"Do you always walk up behind people like that?" I asked him.

He laughed. "If I want to meet them, I do."

It seemed to me like an overly bold thing to say. At the same time, it seemed entirely possible that people did meet like this. I didn't know. In Oregon, there weren't that many new people to meet.

"Paco!" a woman yelled. She was standing outside an upstairs apartment, next to a small, diaper-clad child of indeterminate sex. She had two trash bags in her hands, but she managed to shake her fist at Paco and to say something in Spanish that I didn't understand.

"I'm busy, Ma," Paco said, but he walked back up the steps. He took the bags from the woman and let her kiss his cheek. He started across the yard, trash bags in hand, but before he turned the corner, he gave half a wave to me. He tossed his hand over his shoulder like he was throwing something for me to catch.

He had a lot of nerve, asking me if I was wishing for him, then disappearing like that. He could have at least waited for an answer. He was too smooth. Not my type at all, no way, but I found myself thinking of him long after he had walked away. He had nice eyes, after all, with long black lashes. And really, I didn't have any type, or none that I knew of yet.

When my mother returned, she was smiling. The rainbow scarf that had held her hair up throughout most of the trip had come undone. It hung loose now, off her shoulder. The effect of this, or of the thin, bright air of the place, made her look young.

"Well, it's done," she said. "We are now official residents of Los Angeles."

"Great," I said.

I must have sounded more enthusiastic than she'd expected because she stopped walking and looked at me skeptically. "Great? Just a second ago, you didn't like it."

I looked at the spot where the boy had disappeared. I was already thinking about seeing him again. And the complex did, on second thought, have some good points. It was plain enough to escape notice, and the top floor balcony ran in two directions. In a bad situation, a person at least would have a choice.

"It's okay," I said. "I guess."

We expected a lock, but when we pushed it, the door to Apartment 3 flew open. It was too dark to see much, but right away, I smelled it: dust and old carpet. Cat pee. Long, white telltale hairs covered the welcome mat and the patch of rug beside the door.

"I'm out of here," I said. Cats made my eyes burn. I could feel them puffing up, twitching already. I turned, but she put her arm out to stop me.

"We already paid for the first three months."

I turned. "With what?" I didn't really expect an answer. She'd talk or she wouldn't. It didn't do any good to ask her questions, but she surprised me.

"This and that," she said. "But mostly the old man."

He had buried something then. It was just as I'd thought.

We spent the rest of the evening unpacking and cleaning. Our belongings, when we laid them out, made a shockingly small pile on the living room floor.

"It seems like we might have forgotten a couple things," my mother joked, but I didn't have the heart to laugh.

We are not our things. I knew this, but still, I felt reduced. I felt whittled away.

"Shh," I told her. "Unpack quietly."

She poked a bag of shoes with the broken tip of an umbrella and a tarot card fell out: the Five of Cups.

"The Six of Cups reversed," she announced. "The things we hold up from our past will block our future."

"Except it was the five," I snapped.

She squinted down at it. "It is. Would you look at that!"

"You lie about the stupidest things," I told her.

She went back to unpacking, and I bent down to pick up an old mason jar. The label had curled up on one side, but at one time it had said, OUR LADY OF THE WELL BLESSED SPIRIT WATER $5.52. We'd sold dozens of jars just like it last summer, after my mother paid two ten-year-old boys to tell everyone in town they'd seen an apparition of the Virgin Mary hovering above our well. I unscrewed the lid and held it up to my nose. The dank, river stone smell of Oregon swirled up and floated away.

I put the jar down and poked around some more, looking for my jewelry box, but my heart wasn't in it. It felt as though we were always sifting through ruin, always searching for something we couldn't find, so I picked up my Moon Sign notebook and walked out to the balcony. I leaned over the railing and looked up at the sky. The Perseid meteor shower was at its peak, but I wouldn't be able to see any of it through the haze.

I put the notebook away and traced the Milky Way with my finger. These stars, my mother once told me, were the cattle that the Gemini twins, Castor and Pollux, stole. They combined forces with two of their cousins to commit the crime, but then they all fought over how to divide the spoils. The cousins snuck off with the cattle, and Castor and Pollux ambushed them. In the fight that broke out, Castor died. He went down to Hades, and Pollux went up to Olympus. They couldn't bear to be separated, so Zeus took mercy on them and cast them out into the sky. I'd always liked that story. Gemini was our sign, my mother's and mine, so we were partial to it.

A whistling sound wafted up, and I leaned over the balcony railing. Paco was walking by below. He passed a potted plant and circled the tarp-covered pool before he started down the path to the parking lot. I watched the back of his jacket as he walked to what I assumed was his car, the letters RCCS getting smaller and smaller until they disappeared.

*RCCS*, I thought. *What school is that?*

As I watched his car pull out, I had this crazy urge to run after him, to open the car door and duck inside, into the loud thump of the music he'd turned on, and just go. The balcony railing shook as he drove away.

I didn't see Paco again for almost a week, although I looked for him every day. Then one morning, he appeared behind me in a blur of sun at the top of the metal steps.

"You know you've got a bee on your arm," he shouted down to me.

I was stomping around in a clump of black-eyed Susans, looking for a spot to stake our psychic reading sign, and when he spoke, I jumped. I don't know which thing surprised me more, the bee or him. Neither one seemed completely real. I shifted my arm carefully to let the bee fly away and dropped the sign.

"Are you sure you want to put it there?" He pointed at the bottom of the steps. "Next to the bees' nest?"

There was something soft about his eyes, the long eyelashes, maybe, that didn't seem to go with the rest of his face. For a second, I forgot what he was talking about, but then I said, "I think so. Yes."

He looked at me for what felt like a second or two too long. Then he walked down the steps to the sign and picked it up. I waited while he read it. I expected him to laugh or to make fun of it in some way, but he didn't say anything. He just pushed it into the ground. Then he smacked his arm and said, "Ouch."

"Did you get stung?" I asked. I felt a little bit bad about it. It seemed like my fault.

"Nah," he said. He pulled the stinger out and dropped it on the ground.

"Well," I said, "thanks."

I stole a sideways look at him. He was still looking at the sign, but now he was holding his hand over his arm.

"Was it actually supposed to hang?" he asked, finally.

"It can hang or stand."

"Oh," he said.

We stood for a second, not speaking, while the yard buzzed around us in a bright jumble of bees and flowers and sun. I still wasn't used to the light here, the way it heightened colors and flattened them at the same time. A palm frond dropped between us, and I squinted at Paco's shirt. It had a picture of a leprechaun in running shoes jumping over a sign that said 1ST ANNUAL ST. PATRICK'S DAY JOG-A-THON RCCS. I thought back to his jacket. He'd had the letters RCCS on that, too.

"Is that your school?" I asked.

"What?"

"RCCS. On your shirt."

"Oh, that." He paused, and a bee buzzed around his ear. "Yeah. It's the Rock Canyon Christian School. Where do you go?"

My mother had mentioned the public school, L.A. Unified, but I said, "I think my mother is signing me up for your school. Depending on the price, that is."

"You're in luck, then," he said. "It's dirt cheap. A church runs it."

"Well, I guess I'm going, then," I said.

We said goodbye, and I watched him round the corner, repeating the name of the school on his jacket in my mind: Rock Canyon Christian School. Rock Canyon Christian School.

After he left, I experienced a sudden burst of energy. I bounced around the balcony, watering dead plants, wiping the table, and silently replaying every word either one of us had said.

When my mother walked outside, she said, "What's gotten into you?"

"I found a school," I told her. "It's called the Rock Canyon Christian School."

She looked at me suspiciously. "I thought you were going to L.A. Unified."

"I did, too," I said.

She looked at me in an odd way, but she agreed to call.

"Hello? Hello?" she began in her standard way of leaving a message, but then she surprised me by praising the school and summarizing our financial situation very nicely. Really, I felt almost proud of her. It might have come off as a professional message, had she not, halfway through the call, disintegrated into whiny neediness and begged for a scholarship. She wrapped up the whole show by shouting, "Praise the Lord!" and singing "Amazing Grace" off key.

I felt almost startled when she hung up. It seemed like a crazy kind of call for the school to get on a summer morning, but I told myself to remain optimistic.

"Maybe they'll feel sorry for me," I said. "My mother's so crazy and all."

"We can only hope for the best," she chirped.

# FIVE

My letter of acceptance from RCCS arrived two weeks later, and the following Monday, I started school. My mother dropped me off; she parked sideways in the bus zone so no one could pass us, and we both stared up at the building. It was a large L-shaped structure with white stucco walls and a short sloped orange roof. In front of the main building, surrounded by cactus plants and scattered purple flowers, stood a hill and a cloth-draped cross of weathered wood. A sign above the front door said, YOU HAVE COME TO A JOYFUL GATHERING OF ANGELS. HEBREWS 12:22.

"Go ahead," she said, nudging me. "I'm not parked right."

"In a second," I said.

I just didn't feel ready to go. I looked down at my lap, at the paperwork that Documents for a New Life had given me. There was a sealed transcript from a school in New Hampshire that had burned down, but I wasn't sure what was in the other envelope. What if nothing was in it at all? I held it up to the window, trying to see through it.

"Give that to me," my mother said. She tried to grab the envelope, but I held it tight.

"What will you do with it if I do?" I said.

"I'll rip it open. I'm sick of all your worrying."

Ripping it open would ruin the very official seal that Documents for a New Life had embossed on the front. I held it up to the sun again, but I couldn't see much. Just a few squiggly lines, and the faint outline of yet another seal.

"You can't have it, then," I said.

She settled back in her seat. "You know what? We should have a meeting spot in place."

"You were just thinking that?" I said.

"If the police come, say, while you're at school, meet me at the end of the Santa Monica Pier."

I hadn't been listening very closely but when she said the word *police*, she had my full attention. "Why the pier?" I asked.

She shrugged, rolled down the window, and threw something out. "I just picked it. Does there always have to be a reason?"

I looked up at the school, at the crowd of strangers shuffling in, and, suddenly, I wanted nothing more than to turn around and to go back home with her.

"What are you doing today?" I asked.

She looked surprised. "Me? I don't know. Well, I do know, actually. I have a job."

"You have a job?"

She nodded. "I start today. Look, I've got the ad here." She took it out of her purse and passed it to me. It said: "Work from home: The Tarot Hotline needs telephone psychics." The job was filed under Jobs for Actors.

"This looks good," I said.

She looked pleased, as though I'd paid her a great compliment. "Well, someone's got to pay for the school."

The school wasn't going to cost us much. I'd qualified for a scholarship, but I didn't say anything about it. I wanted to encourage her.

"Right, thanks," I said.

"And you haven't even heard the best part. They're giving us cell phones."

"Me too?" It didn't make sense.

"Well, no. But I'm buying you one, so you can help me out."

This was an exciting development. I'd always wanted a cell phone. I tried not to think about what "help out" might mean. I cheered and hugged her until someone honked.

She leaned out the window and yelled, "All right, already!" Then, more nicely, to me, "You better go."

I gathered my backpack and stepped out. When I turned around to look for her, the car was gone.

Inside, I walked down the hall until I came to the office— a small, dark, windowed box at the center of the school. I waited in a plastic chair beneath a painting of an angel on the Santa Monica Pier until a middle-aged woman in a pantsuit waved me in. She had dark hair, pulled back into a bun, a pointed chin, and thick tortoise shell glasses. She pulled something out of a long file cabinet and sat back down at her desk.

"I'm Ms. Jones," she said, "the principal here. And you must be the new scholarship student."

I nodded.

"Not that it matters," she said. "I mean, you shouldn't feel different."

"I don't," I said.

"That's good," she said. "You shouldn't." She looked down at her papers, flipped one over. "The donor who provides the scholarships, Joan Fields, will be here at an assembly in three weeks. You'll have the opportunity to thank her then."

I hadn't known that a specific church person had provided my scholarship, but it made sense. I said, "Okay."

"Because it's very important that you thank her."

I nodded. I could see that she thought it was. I handed her my transcripts and held my breath as she opened them up.

"A's. For the most part," she said. "A few B's."

I'd been hoping for straight A's, so this was disappointing. This version wasn't as good as my real transcript. She must have thought I was feeling bad about my school burning down, because she said, "I'm sorry to hear about your school. Such a tragedy."

I nodded. It was, I supposed. For someone.

She crossed her arms and tapped the floor with her high-heeled shoe. She's not buying it, I thought. Did she know? I considered leaving, just taking off at a run. The principal didn't look fast, and she was wearing heels. She'd have to throw them off to have any shot at catching me.

"Is there a problem?" I asked, finally.

She leaned forward. "There is. It's your purse."

I looked down at it. It was just a brown bag; it didn't look like anything special to me. My mother had given it to me as a gift for starting school, to make up, I guess, for dragging me to L.A. in the first place. It hadn't really worked, and I didn't have much of an opinion about it either way. I'd assumed, up until now, that she had bought it at Wal-Mart, like everything else.

"It's a designer bag," she said. "We don't allow designer bags at this school. That purse you have there is worth at least eight hundred dollars."

"Eight hundred dollars?" I nearly choked. My mother stole it, then. There was no other explanation.

The principal eyed me suspiciously. "Dump it out. I'm confiscating it."

I wasn't about to let it go that easily, not now that I knew it was worth eight hundred dollars. I scrambled around for something to say.

"My mother gave me this purse after the fire," I said, quickly. "To make me feel better. It's kind of important to me."

The principal's face softened. She took on the concerned look she'd had earlier, when we'd discussed the imaginary school fire. "It's okay for today," she said. "You didn't know the rule. Just keep it in your locker."

The rest of the morning passed without incident. I found my classes without much problem, my locker opened, and at second period study hall, I sold my designer purse to a girl for two hundred and twenty dollars.

The girl had a pale face, small, burrowed eyes, and short, asymmetrical, blond hair. She wore a pair of black lace-up boots instead of the regulation loafers, and a black T-shirt peeked out from beneath her white button-down shirt. She was applying makeup out of a small handheld compact when she noticed me, but she put it down and walked over with one eye done. She looked lopsided, but not unfriendly. Not at first. Or, not completely. In fact, in the brief second or two before she spoke, I thought she might have walked over to welcome me to my new school. The principal had told me that I would soon meet a "friendly person from the student welcome committee who would show me around," and I had yet to see this person.

"So," the girl said, "you're that new girl."

I nodded. A bell rang. The start of second period. Locker doors slammed up and down the hall, but the girl stayed still. She let the crowd walk around her while she studied me in a disdainful way. The friendly person the principal spoke of must have hidden from me or must not have existed. She was certainly not this girl.

"Paco told me about you," she said.

"Yeah?" I said. I was interested now. I couldn't help it.

"So, what?" She leaned back against her locker, propped her foot behind her. "Can I touch your bag?"

It was an odd request, but not an overly difficult one, so I said, "Sure, go ahead."

I held my purse out to her, and she extended her hand to pat it gently, the way you might touch a baby or a small animal.

"It's real," she said. "I can always tell."

"I'll sell it to you, if you want," I told her.

She liked that idea. She left and came back with two hundred and twenty dollars in her hand. I didn't know what kind of girl kept two hundred dollars in her locker, but I was pleased with the sum. It was a tidy profit when you considered my mother must have stolen it.

"You can't tell anyone where I got it," she said.

"Okay," I agreed.

An expression—anger, irritation, recognition . . . I wasn't sure what—sped across her face just before she slung my purse over her shoulder and walked away.

After a couple steps, she turned around and said, "You don't really look the way he said you did."

How did Paco say I looked? I almost asked, but I didn't want to look too interested.

"Well, that happens sometimes," I said.

"Paco and I are really good friends," she said. "I mean, *really* good friends."

"That's great for you two."

As soon as she disappeared, I remembered that I'd left a lipstick and my mother's Ryder Waite tarot deck inside the purse. I could replace the lipstick. The color had looked better in the drugstore, anyway, but the deck was her favorite. *Oh, well*, I thought. I wasn't about to ask for it back.

It turned out I did get the deck back. The second I sat down in my next class, the girl I'd sold my purse to flung it at me.

"Lose something?" she said.

The deck brushed my shoulder and scattered to the floor. It took me a while to gather all the cards. When I finished, I looked around for the girl. She was standing three rows down from me, wearing my lipstick, or a very similar shade of pink.

"Thanks," I said. "You can keep the lipstick. Oh, I see you did."

She sat down at her desk. After a while, she leaned forward. "Are you some kind of psychic reader freak?"

"It's just an old deck I had. It's nothing."

I'd thought I might actually be able to keep the psychic reading business a secret here, but it looked like I hadn't managed to, even for one day. The girl studied my face for a second, but then she turned around. She was going to let it drop. I tried not to look too relieved. I followed the direction of her eyes and saw Paco walking through the doorway. He had his backpack flung over one shoulder, and it hit against the sides of chairs as he maneuvered down the row. His hair was short, neat, his shoes polished, but his shirt was partway open, un-tucked in the sloppy way of the braver boys. The tie the school made him wear hung out from the front zipper pocket of his backpack.

He sat down, but just before he did, he glanced over at me. I was certain of it. Our eyes met, but then I turned away. I looked out the window and watched a man in a maintenance uniform pass by, his body jiggling on the seat of a riding mower. The engine made an aching sound when he turned the corner, and the smell of hot, tossed grass wafted up to mix with the scent of eraser dust.

"Where'd you get this bag, Sydney?" someone squealed behind me.

Her name was Sydney, then. I'd wondered what it was.

"Neiman Marcus," she said. "Where do you think?"

She looked at me crossways. She must have been afraid I might disagree. In the brief second that she turned away, she lost the purse. A boy in a baseball cap grabbed it and flipped it to another boy. That boy flipped it to Paco, who flipped it to a fourth boy. It went around the class like that for several minutes, while Sydney shrieked and hopped after it like a monkey.

When the teacher walked in, the purse fell to the floor. The boys climbed off the tops of their desks and the class turned to face him.

Mr. Aimes was somewhere in his late thirties, very thin, with short brown hair that stood practically straight up. He walked around the classroom with a long stick, something that looked like it came from a drum set, but longer and fatter. He used this stick to point to the board, to his subject of the day, and tell us that he hoped we would discuss it with him. He said *hoped*, I learned later, because sometimes no one did. If this happened, he'd have the discussion with himself, alone, something that bothered him a great deal less than you would expect.

It didn't take Mr. Aimes long to notice a designer purse had invaded his classroom. It was in his hands the second Sydney scooped it off the floor. He consulted his chart, a sheet that detailed the markings of designer purses. He studied it like a geometry problem, at different angles, before he turned it right side up. He looked completely dumfounded. He was a man in a wide, striped tie—a man who had this morning managed to almost, but not quite, match his own clothes. Identifying a designer purse was clearly more than he could manage.

"Louis Vuitton?" he said, unsure.

"No," Sydney said. "Definitely not."

He scratched his head. Clearly, he was not in any way sure about his decision, but he didn't let this stop him. He dumped the contents of the purse on Sydney's lap, dropped the purse in his top drawer, and turned the key.

"One less symbol of a materialistic society in this world," he said.

I told my mother about the purse while we ate dinner that night. We were sitting in the new, cramped kitchen in the dark, beside a tiny open window. The lights were off; the room one shade darker than the air outside. We'd told ourselves it was to conserve electricity, but really, I think, it was to remind us of home, of our dinners in our dark garage.

"One less symbol of a materialistic society in the world," my mother repeated. "What a great line! But wait, the teacher took it?" She paused, her Sizzler Steak House glass in midair.

I couldn't tell her I'd sold her gift, so I nodded.

She didn't say anything else about it because a sound on the steps outside had distracted her. She leaned over the table and pushed her head out the open window.

"Get off of our steps!" She slammed her fist down on the windowsill. "Get off!"

The steps weren't really ours, but they were in front of our apartment, so in her mind we owned them. She wanted the people in the rest of the complex to use the other steps, which were much farther away, so she set the chairs up in front of our apartment like a gate. I looked out the window. The culprit was halfway down now, and he looked like Paco. He had the same springy walk, the same short, black hair.

"I'm going to start charging a toll," my mother went on. "I swear that same boy was standing out there listening to me today. Or, it could have been the police." She began to pace the floor. "Do you think the phone is tapped?"

I rolled my eyes. "The phone is not tapped," I said. I stood and started for the door.

"It's too late to go out," she said.

I walked out to the balcony, anyway, and slid the door shut behind me. The night was warm. Traffic had slowed to a rustle, and the garden looked silver. The flowers made sharp, black silhouettes against the sky. I leaned over the balcony railing and looked down, but I didn't see Paco. I couldn't help feeling disappointed, but I decided it was for the best. Whatever would I say to him? I wanted to say, "This girl named Sydney said you were talking about me. Were you? What did you say?" but of course, I couldn't ask him that.

"Hey, you," someone said. I looked in the direction of the voice and spotted Paco on the other side of the balcony. He was standing near the railing, holding a tube of paint and a long fat brush that looked like a squirrel's tail. The light from his door made a bright rectangle around the easel in front of him.

"Hey," I said.

"So I hear you guys bought the steps when you moved in."

"Yeah," I said. "About that. You can use them."

"A lady in a bathrobe and hair curlers says otherwise."

"She's kind of a crazy person," I said. "You have to ignore her."

He smiled. He had a great smile—sudden and wide. It took over his whole face, as if it had gripped him suddenly and refused to let him go.

"That's kind of what I thought," he said. "What is she, exactly? Some kind of fortune-teller?"

"Something like that," I said.

He laughed.

"It's kind of a family business," I admitted. "We do it together." He was going to find out, anyway, living next door. I figured I might as well admit to it.

He considered this. "That's cool," he said finally. He picked up a smaller brush and leaned toward the canvas, squinting at some small detail on the other side. For a while, we were quiet, then he said, "You know, I think it might be against the law to call people up the way she does."

I didn't know what he was talking about. The customers for the Tarot Hotline were supposed to call her, not the other way around. "What do you mean, she calls people up?" I asked.

"Well, when I walked by your window today, I heard her leave a message on someone's machine. She said she had urgent news. She said she'd had a premonition that something bad would happen if the person didn't call her back right away."

I thought about this. It didn't sound legal to me, either. It sounded problematic, but it wasn't something I wanted to discuss with him right then, so I said, "I try not to notice what she's up to. It works out better that way."

He laughed. He must have thought I was joking. He went back to painting, but after a while he said, "How do you like the school?"

"It's okay," I said. "What are you painting?"

"Guess," he said.

My guess was that it was a self-portrait. He seemed like the kind of person who might do that. In his self-portrait, he'd look larger than life. He'd have bigger arms or a wider chest, a cape, like Superman. He'd figure out a way to make himself into a hero.

If I could paint, I'd paint things as they are. I'd paint Los Angeles in all her entirety. Her gritty streets as well as her clean ones. Her poor, as well as her rich. If I made her into a person, I'd give her a beautiful face. A high, proud face, with good cheekbones and movie star eyes, but I'd age her a little bit. I'd make it clear, in my painting, that she wouldn't look as good up close as she did in pictures. When I finished, I'd give her some wings. I'd have to, because of her name, but the wings would be black, more like a bat than an angel. If I added a halo, I'd make it faint. The gold would look yellow, the ring like a ring of smog.

"It's our humble home. The Sepulveda Apartment complex."

"Why would you paint that?" I asked.

He shrugged. "It's as good a subject as any other apartment complex."

He turned the canvas toward me and I stared, dumbfounded, at the Sepulveda complex, in all its aged beauty, with its twisted gray stone path and its sun-struck windows. Its yard of tangled flowers rose up in the form of bright smiling kites to twist on the highway above.

"I like it," I said.

He frowned. "You sound surprised."

"I didn't mean it that way. I didn't mean I didn't think your painting would be good. I just meant . . ." I didn't finish. It wasn't the fact that the painting was good that had surprised me. In fact, when I looked at it again, I decided that it wasn't that good. The colors clashed, and the lines looked imprecise. The smiles on the flower kites bled a little too freely into the sky. No, the thing that took my breath away had to do with the apartment itself. The way it leaned or glowed or shook multicolored kites up from its lawn. It's truly astonishing, the way that two people can look at the same place and see an entirely different thing.

"Are those kites or flowers?" I asked.

He frowned. "They're bobbing heads."

"Oh," I said. "I see." I thought I might be distracting him from his work, so I started to walk away.

"Go ahead and use the steps all you want," I said.

"You're leaving?" he called back. "Hey . . ."

I turned back around.

He paused, like he'd forgotten what he meant to say. Finally, he said, "Don't be a stranger. Okay?"

"Okay," I said. I shut the door to my apartment and smiled in the dark.

# SIX

The following Monday, I arrived at school two minutes after the bell rang. The hall was empty, quiet enough to echo. My sneakers made a squeaking sound on the shiny floor. I turned the corner and followed the row of blue lockers to mine. Sydney was sitting there, slouched down with earphones on, her back against the door. She had a big, black windbreaker jacket on that covered her knees so that she looked very thin and small, and she wore a fat silver chain around her neck. Her hair was pulled up into a short, spiked tail. She glared at me when I walked past.

"The bag is gone," she said. "I want my money back."

"I don't do refunds," I said. It wasn't my fault she'd lost the purse. I saw Mr. Aimes again in my head. The tired, determined way he'd looked at the purse as he plucked it up. I heard the satisfying slam his desk drawer had made when he'd locked the bag in. I tried not to smile, but I couldn't help it. I shook my locker door until she moved slightly to the side, then I opened it.

"I think this is yours," she said. She reached into her jacket pocket and pulled out my lipstick tube. Just the tube. I opened it up and rolled up air.

"Thanks," I said. I tossed it into my locker and slammed the door. "Excuse me."

I stepped over her foot and started down the hall.

"Penalty is detention for skipping or tardy," she called after me. "You're stupid to go."

I went to my first three classes, then I ate lunch outside by myself. I leaned up against a eucalyptus tree and took small bites of my peanut butter sandwich. I watched an ant circle a blade of grass and a ladybug climb a soda can. The bugs were my main entertainment, but also, occasionally, I looked over at Paco. He was sitting in front of a large circular fountain with his back to me beside a heavyset blond girl and a boy with glasses. There was something about the close, sprawled out way they leaned toward each other that depressed me. In Oregon, I'd never exactly been popular—the psychic reading business had pretty much guaranteed that—but I'd generally had a date to whatever dance or event came up, and I'd always had friends. I'd never had to eat alone.

I took my Moon Sign notebook out of my backpack and flipped through it for something to do. The page opened to the day before school started when I'd written:

*Bright waxing moon in a clear sky. Can signify a new and exciting change.*

It seemed silly to me now that I'd ever been hopeful, and I had to shut the book. I left the courtyard before the bell rang and stood outside the door to my next class.

I returned from school to find my mother walking squat-legged across the balcony, struggling to push an additional potted plant in front of the steps.

"Customers stampeding you today?" I asked her, although I thought I knew the answer from the silly thing she was doing and from the sloppy way she was dressed.

"Right," she said. "A big, giant mob of zero."

I sighed. It was disappointing, but it didn't surprise me. Los Angeles, while a good place to hide, wasn't a particularly good place to start a psychic reading business. People love psychics in Los Angeles. They like anything New Age, anything that has to do even remotely with the paranormal, but unfortunately, the market for all this is pretty much saturated. A man out in Hollywood made a fortune off changing people's negative auras at living room parties, and a Doctor Doolittle–type person talked to animals. A number of people claimed communion with beings on other planets, and those people were hard to compete with. As for tarot card readers, we were a dime a dozen.

Still, we gave it our best shot. We'd check the newspaper for star spottings and map our attack. We'd spend our evenings in front of the Westwood Theater, leaning over ropes at movie premiers, dangling our business cards like candy. Or we'd hang around Rodeo Drive and wait. Occasionally, we'd spot someone. Sometimes, they'd take our card. More often than not, the outing would end in dismal failure.

My mother thought the problem with business was me: I let people get away. I complained too much. I was ready to go home practically as soon as we got there. And I thought the problem was her: most of her star sightings turned out to be tourists—people who, when approached, laughed or looked shocked or just plain scared. Every one of them vehemently denied being a celebrity of any type. My mother never believed them. A scene generally ensued. It might be large or small, loud or just silly, but the outcome was always the same. It never, even once, ended with us getting one single movie star client.

My mother spun the plant around so the crack in the pot wouldn't show, and backed up to admire her work. "I found it beside the trashcan," she said.

"Good for you," I said. I started inside, but she stopped me.

"There was another one, too. Hey, can you man the phone line for me for one second, so I can grab it?"

"No way," I said.

The phone rang and she walked off. She knew I would answer it. We both knew it was more important to me that she keep her job than it was to her.

"Hello," I said hesitantly. Sometimes, the Tarot Hotline scared me. You never knew what sort of person might call.

"That you, Lindsey?" a crackly voice said. It was only Edna, a woman who had quickly become one of our regulars. She called from time to time, whenever she lost her false teeth.

"It's me," I said.

"Would it kill you to call your mother sometimes?"

"I'm sorry," I said. It was best, when she confused me with her daughter, to just apologize for everything. Otherwise she ranted. I sat down on the plastic balcony chair and propped up my feet on the railing. Below me, in the courtyard, a man drummed out a song on a hubcap, and a boy kicked a soccer ball against the wall.

"Young people," Edna clucked. "So, tell me, am I warm?"

We often played that children's game where one person says warm or cold as the other one wanders around the room, looking for a hidden item. I didn't mind. The game was okay as games go, although in this case, it seemed painfully pointless. I had not hidden her false teeth and therefore did not have any information about them at all.

"Where are you?" I asked.

"In the bathtub," she called out in the peculiar, slurred annunciation of the temporarily toothless.

"It sounds like you're running the water," I said. "You're not standing in the tub, are you?"

"Yes," she said. "Warm or cold?"

"I think you should get out of the tub."

Splashing sounds, then, "But I remove my teeth sometimes with a red cup, and there's a red cup, here, in the tub."

"You should turn off the water," I said.

More splashing noises. "But the teeth are the color of the bottom."

In some odd way, what she'd said almost made sense. I considered hanging up the phone. Edna didn't sound like she had a lot of money to call the Tarot line, and I worried about that. On the other hand, I worried about her safety if I let her go. We don't owe our customers anything; they pay us. That's what my mother always said, but I never completely believed it. It's always seemed to me that if someone asks for your help, you should give it, or at least admit that you can't. Otherwise, you really aren't fit to walk the Earth. It was a flaw in our business model that came up occassionally.

"My tarot cards say that you will not find your teeth in the tub," I told Edna.

"Why, here they are," she said. "In the tub. My teeth!"

"Well, there you go."

I breathed a sigh of relief, but then she whispered, "Oh gracious, I've lost my teeth again."

After she hung up, I couldn't stop thinking about her. There was something about her voice, some hollow or confused quality that struck me as both disturbingly weird and shockingly familiar. I pictured her at home, in an apartment not unlike ours. A little old lady with a phone in her hand, on an endless search for her elusive teeth. She's just old, I told myself. Senile. But then, I thought, what if it happened because everyone left her? At one point, she'd had a daughter, too.

I watched my mother roll the flowerpot through the courtyard and up the steps and thought, what if it's true? What if the world is wild, liquid, moving? If nothing is solid; it just appears to be so?

# SEVEN

The next afternoon, my mother stole someone's wallet. I returned home from school to find her at the kitchen table, squinting at it in a surprised way. When she saw me, she shrugged. She dumped the whole thing out on the table and we stared at the contents: a handful of money, a large collection of credit cards, a stick of gum, two gift cards, and a movie stub.

"Wow," I said. "You actually stole this."

She must have thought it was a compliment because she said, "It wasn't that hard. It was kind of falling out of his pocket. I just snapped it up."

The license inside the wallet said that it belonged to someone named Reginald Clay, forty-four years old, a man with bushy eyebrows, thin lips, and a blank expression. I couldn't help but feel sorry for him. His long face had a resigned quality about it. He looked like he might be the sort of person who was always running into women who stole his wallet.

"You actually stole this," I said again.

We kept the money (it amounted to fifty-eight dollars) and a gift card to a restaurant called Chez Marc, but we mailed the rest of it back to the address on the driver's license.

"Thanks for dinner at Chez Marc!" my mother wrote on the envelope in her uptilted, sprawling hand. "We wish you well!"

"Cross out the last part," I said. "He'll never believe it."

She looked surprised. "But we do wish him well. I do, anyway. Now, go send it."

It took me a while to put the wallet in the box. If I mailed it, we would be pickpockets. A brand new low. I spent a minute or two weighing the pros and cons of it, but in the end, I dropped it in. It didn't seem all that much different than anything else we'd already done.

We took the gift card she'd stolen and that night we went to Chez Marc. We were both excited about it. We'd read in a tour guide that it was a great place to spot movie stars. If we were going to be Hollywood psychics to the stars, it would help, we both thought, if we actually met a star.

Chez Marc was in Beverly Hills. It had valet parking, but we didn't use it. We parked in the garage across the street. I watched with reservation as my mother took a ticket from the man in the booth. My mother never could be trusted with tickets. Once, she lost a restaurant validation in the time it took us to travel down four floors in an elevator, and another time she lost a movie ticket in the two minutes it took to cross the movie theater lobby. Parking garage tickets always provided the hardest challenge for her and are also, unfortunately, the most important to hang on to. If you lose a parking garage ticket, I know from experience, you have to pay the highest rate possible, the whole day usually, even if you just parked in the lot for half an hour. This policy, whenever it came up, never failed to surprise and outrage my mother. A mad search for the parking ticket would ensue, followed by a long, loud scene in which she tried but failed to explain away the situation to the parking attendant. This time, I took the ticket from her as soon as I saw it and put it in my own pocket.

We crossed the street and walked in the door. A man in a tuxedo took our names and our thrift store coats and assured us that chances were very high we would see a star.

"Tourists?" he asked.

"Business women," my mother said. The man nodded politely and looked over her shoulder.

When the hostess took us to our seats, my mother said, "She put us very close to the kitchen. I'm going to ask to move."

"Don't do it," I said. I didn't like it when she changed our table in restaurants. I wanted her to be happy with whatever, like everyone else. I picked up the menu, but everything on it was in French. A blank column of air ran down the side in the spot where the prices should be.

"We'll just move a little bit. To that table there. It's empty. I don't think anyone will mind."

"I'll mind," I said, but she was already standing. She took two steps forward, but a couple beat her to it. They sat down and the hostess handed them two menus.

"Did you see her?" my mother said, sitting back down. "The woman who just sat down. She's someone. You know what? I think a movie star just took our table."

"I don't recognize her," I said.

"You need glasses, Lindsey. You really do. Look at her. Now, she is somebody."

I looked back at the woman. She had red hair, piled at the top of her head, and she was wearing a tight green dress. I tried to remember if we'd seen her in any of the magazines we'd studied.

"Excuse me," my mother said to a waiter—not our waiter.

"Yes, ma'am," he said. He stopped in front of us, a full tray of drinks balanced on his forearm. "Would you like me to get your server for you?"

"Oh, no. You'll do just fine. Just a quick question. Who is that woman at the table by the window?"

The waiter leaned in, his drinks tipping but not spilling. "Miriam DeFalco," he whispered. "From the movie *Beauticians and Gorillas*. But you didn't hear it from me."

He walked off, and my mother turned to me. "*Beauticians and Gorillas*! Didn't see that one. But I knew she was someone. I have a kind of radar, like that. I know how to spot a star. If the waiter comes when I'm gone, just order dessert. It turns out we only have twenty-five dollars on the card."

"Tell me what you're going to do before you do it," I said, but I shouldn't have bothered. She was already up and halfway across the room.

I sat at the table by myself, long enough to drink a soda and to order and eat what appeared to be an ice cream crepe, but then my curiosity got the better of me. I moved my chair to the other side of the table to get a better look.

At second glance, I did recognize the woman. I'd seen her in one or another of my mother's magazines. One of the articles, if I recalled correctly, had said she was fading out of the limelight. She was riddled with personal trauma and soon to become yesterday's news, but to see her you wouldn't know it. She sat very tall and straight with her legs crossed, and she moved her arm across the table in an elegant way. A slice of slim white thigh poked out from the slit of her dress.

"Bravo," she said when my mother threw a deck of cards through the air in front of her. It looked to me as though things were going at least halfway well, but then Miriam whispered something to her friend and both of them laughed. A throaty, mean, jumbled together laugh. It swirled around the restaurant before it settled on top of my mother. I felt my heart deflate. We should never have come to California. It was a mistake.

The maître d' walked up to Miriam's table and picked up the tarot cards. "Excuse me," he said to my mother. "I'm going to have to ask you to leave the restaurant."

"I'm a paying guest," my mother said.

"Your check will be waiting for you outside." He stretched out his long arm and pointed at the door.

It was time to leave. I dumped the basket of bread in my purse and stood, but my mother didn't move.

"I'll just finish up this reading, first," she said. "Miriam wants me to, don't you?"

"I think you should leave," Miriam said.

The maître d' touched my mother on the arm and tried to steer her to the door, but she shook him off. She walked out by herself, demonstrating to him, and to all who looked on, the long, elegant strides she'd perfected at the Miss America Pageant. "That's me," my mother had whispered the night we'd watched the video. "Can you believe it?" How proud she had been, walking like that, smiling with her whole face, her whole heart! The crowd had clapped for her, smiled for her, loved her. It had broken my heart to watch it because I knew the outcome. I knew she wasn't going to be the one carrying the roses.

Tonight, she walked out of the restaurant like a person in charge. I felt proud, watching her. It didn't matter that the maître d' thudded along behind her. Anyone looking on would think that he was the ridiculous one.

"What a nut!" Miriam DeFalco said. "People like that should not be allowed to walk the streets." She leaned back and laughed, and with her mouth wide open, she did not look pretty anymore.

"Your movie sucked," I told her as I walked by. "And you don't look as good in person. Just thought you should know."

She didn't say anything, so I walked out the door. I spotted my mother immediately, hiding behind a potted plant.

"Forget the car," she said. "We have to run. They're getting our check. The gift card's expired." She stepped out from behind the plant, still holding one of the branches, and gathered up her shoes. She did a little dance as she ran. "Faster, faster," she said, as she darted down the street.

I ran after her, but I was laughing too hard to go very fast. We stepped onto the main street and a woman in a fur coat and a bikini stepped back to let us pass. A teenage boy with a press-on beard waved from the corner. The clunky grandness of the motion encouraged me. For a second, I forgot we'd just been kicked out of a restaurant. I took a step forward, and the crowd skipped a beat to absorb me.

"We're out on Sepulveda," my mother shouted to the people we passed. "Here, take our card." We crossed the street and looped back to the parking garage.

On the way home, we rolled the car windows down and let the night air swirl in around us. My hair blew into my face and stung my eyes, and it became very hard to see my mother. Until the very last moment, when we turned onto Sepulveda, I couldn't say for sure that she was crying.

# EIGHT

The next morning, my mother stayed in bed a little bit later than usual, but she woke up in time to drive me to school.

"Last night was unfortunate," she said when we pulled up. "But it taught me something. Know how you get in with these people?"

"How?" I looked down at her pajama pants. I wondered briefly if she planned to go anywhere after she dropped me off, but I decided I didn't care enough to ask.

"By recommendation. They recommend you. Do you know there's a guy who calls himself the dry cleaner to the stars? It's the same with hairdressers. Same with psychics. If we're going to do this Hollywood psychic thing, we've got to get a recommendation. It's the only way."

I didn't believe it was the only way. One big difference between my mother and me was that I could, in most cases, think of five or six different ways for every "only" way she saw, but I liked the fact that she was getting into it.

"Okay." I put my hand on the car door.

She put her hand on my sleeve to stop me. "Next year you'll be doing your own thing. College and all."

I turned. It was the first time she'd admitted it.

"I mean," she corrected herself, "I know you'll always work with me. We're a team and all that. I know we would never split up, but it wouldn't hurt to have some money squirreled away. Just in case."

She'd thought it too, then. She'd known, all along, that the psychic to the stars thing was for her, to set her up financially so I could go. "You're right," I agreed. "It wouldn't hurt."

She looked down at her lap. The sun on her face made an odd shadow. It hollowed out her eyes in a way that made her face look thin and sad. Looking at her that way, I had the sudden, alarming thought that I was not just leaving for school, but forever. I felt my chest tighten, the way it did sometimes when something awful happened, even though the only thing I'd done was put my hand on the door.

I leaned over and hugged her.

"Well, that was nice, Lindsey. That was nice." She looked so surprised and pleased, it struck me, suddenly, how very little it took to make her happy. I scooped up my backpack and opened the door.

I was halfway down the hall when I ran into Paco.

"Hey, Lindsey." He smiled, and I felt myself smile back. I felt my legs slow, of their own accord, to fall into step with him.

"Hey," I said.

We walked together, past the lockers and around the corner near the gym. Neither one of us spoke. We just walked. I felt a little bit nervous with him. It had been easier to talk to him the other night in the dark. He didn't seem to notice, though.

When we got to his class, he said, "Bye, Lindsey."

I liked the way he said my name. I was replaying it over and over in my head in his voice when I literally ran into Sydney.

"Hello," she said. "Someone's standing here."

"Sorry," I said.

She looked down the hall at Paco, frowned, and turned back to me.

"He's a junior, you know," she said.

"I know," I said.

"You're a senior, right?"

I wasn't sure what she was getting at. One year? Did she think he was too young for me? "Right," I said.

"You know what? You're wearing my old uniform."

"What?"

"My old uniform. On you. See the hole in the skirt. It's a cigarette burn. I recognize it."

I looked down at my skirt, at the small black dot on the hem. I don't know why I hadn't noticed it before. I can be like that, sometimes; I don't always notice things. Once I had a ketchup stain on my shirt all day that I didn't see.

"I'm sorry. I told my mom she shouldn't donate that one to the school." Her voice was apologetic, but loud, too. I could tell she wanted everyone to hear.

A group of girls standing in front of the lockers beside us looked over. I'd seen them before. They were quiet girls, fashionably aloof and sharply vicious, with bright swinging bags and headbands that made a studied pop of color against their gray uniforms. I'd watched them scowl at other girls and pitch their hall passes into bathroom trashcans, but I had, so far, managed to avoid them.

"This was yours?" I told Sydney. "I thought it was stretched out."

It might have been a good comeback . . . if Sydney had weighed more than ninety-three pounds. As it was, it was stupid, but the girls with the bright bags laughed anyway. The sound of it settled around Sydney, diminishing her, until even I started to feel sorry for her.

After Sydney walked away, someone tapped me on the shoulder. It was the pretty, heavyset, blond girl I'd seen the other day sitting with Paco at lunch.

"I don't usually like fat jokes," she said. "But I have to give you that one. That one really hit her where it hurts. I'm Emily, by the way. I'm here on scholarship, too. We're kind of lepers around here, if you haven't figured it out."

"I figured it out," I said.

"We sit together at lunch. You should look for us. Paco sits with us, too."

She paused when she said Paco's name, as if she were waiting for my reaction. How did everyone know how I felt about him?

"Okay," I said. Lunch was the worst part of the day. It was unbearable to think about spending it alone, again, under that tree.

When the lunch bell rang, I found Emily at the far edge of the courtyard, sitting on the grass beside the fountain. When she saw me, she waved. Outside, and on warm days, most people just wore the shirt, but she had the whole button-down sweater on, and her face and neck were flushed. Paco was to her left, leaning back with his face to the sky, beside a junior named Scott, who I recognized from my seniors-only math class. He was a thin, small-boned boy with glasses and a cowlick on the side of his head that looked as if he'd tried to push it down with gel.

"He won't say hi," Emily said about him, when I sat down. "He doesn't believe in greeting people."

"Hi," he said. He looked up from an ancient looking handheld device and smirked at Emily.

Emily rolled her eyes. "It's one of those cheap trivia games. He practices at lunch. We're all very exciting here."

Scott grunted.

"Let me see it," Paco said. He tried to take it away, but Scott held it up and away.

"He's been on three game shows," Emily explained. "He's trying to get on *Millionaire*, but it's hard. He calls every night." She pointed at my brown bag. "Dump out your lunch."

I added my food to the pile between them on the lawn.

"Good," Emily said. "You've got some good stuff."

It didn't look that good to me. It was just a ham sandwich and a Rice Krispies treat, but I was glad it had passed their unknown criteria. I stole a look at Paco. He'd moved a little bit closer to me and was no longer leaning back on the lawn.

"We share our lunches," he explained. "We've been doing it since second grade."

I nodded. I felt funny talking to him, because of the way people kept bringing him up.

Emily looked back and forth between us. "I'll explain it to her." She turned back to me. "If you bring something one day, you put it in. If you don't bring something, that day, it's okay. You can still eat." She didn't say why someone wouldn't have something one day, but I figured I could guess. She split my Rice Krispies treat into four pieces and gave one to me.

I had the feeling someone was staring at me. I turned around, and sure enough, Sydney was looking at me from the other side of the courtyard. She was sitting on the steps with her arms around her knees, glaring at me.

"That girl has it in for me," I told Emily.

"Nah, she's looking at Paco," Emily said. "They used to date."

Paco shrugged.

"Oh," I said. It made sense now. It must have been why she'd frowned when she'd seen me with Paco, why she'd made fun of my uniform.

"I'm just filling her in," Emily told Paco. She turned to me and said, "We've all been together, the same stupid people, since kindergarten."

I stared at her, surprised. I knew they'd all come over from the Rock Canyon Christian Elementary School together, but I didn't know it was a bad thing for anyone but me.

"It's nice to see a new face," she added.

I sat with the scholarship kids at lunch all week. I didn't think about my mother much, or the psychic reading business, or any of our crazy, shoot-the-moon plans. At lunch, on the lawn in the ordinary light, my entire life seemed unreal—a type of costume party, but, if so, one where people wore their real faces and hid their masks. Because (and this sent prickles up and down my spine) when I really stopped to think about it—lunch, the school, my new friends—that was the illusion. I wasn't really Lindsey Smith. She didn't exist, and I, Lindsey Allen, might not even be able to stay.

# NINE

In October, the school held an assembly in the auditorium of the elementary school building next door in honor of our scholarship donor, Joan Fields. Our entire high school walked over together in one giant, colorless procession: gray pants for the boys, gray plaid skirts for the girls. We must have looked like a giant flock of birds, flapping across the street in V formation, with the principal, up front in high heels, breaking up the wind.

"The Santa Annas are here," Emily told me, stepping beside me.

"The what?"

"The devil winds. They blow in off the desert this time of year."

I took a deep breath: Jasmine, and Desert Rose, and car exhaust—a scent as sweet as a candy heart and just as sticky. It stuck in my mouth and in the back of my throat. I coughed until I almost choked, but I couldn't get rid of it.

"They make people go crazy and start fires," she said. "You'll see it soon on the news."

I didn't want to think about fires or the crazy reasons someone might start one. It seemed like I'd already thought about that enough. I stepped away from her, into the cluster of the group, so the wind wouldn't blow my skirt.

We paused in front of the elementary school, and a limo pulled up. A couple of the braver kids tried to peer inside, and one boy knocked on the window. But for the most part, people ignored it. "What are you, a tourist?" was the thing people said around here if you showed any interest in limos.

I didn't want to be labeled as a tourist, but when the others started up the steps, I couldn't help it and turned around. A door opened and a woman in a skirt suit stepped out. She was tall, with a thin, high-boned face, and chin length hair with streaks of bright silver. I had yet to see a woman in L.A., old or otherwise, who had let any part of her hair go gray. She stepped onto the curb and squinted at the sun for a second before she walked inside.

The assembly began with a strings concert. Fifteen or so elementary school–aged kids in black glittery vests took the stage to play a squeaky rendition of "Ode to Joy." When the song ended, the principal asked us to be quiet, which, more or less, we did. The students took their seats, and the woman I'd seen step out of the limo walked up onto the stage. She stepped behind the podium and turned to squint at us. I liked the way she stood, a bit back, her legs slightly apart and her head to the side, studying the uniformed students in front of her the way a person might study a group of ants on a potato chip. I liked the silver streaks in her hair, I decided. It was honest.

She cleared her throat and said, "Thank you for inviting me today."

She tapped the microphone. It seemed to be working, but she tapped it again, anyway. "My late husband, Saul, would have been so pleased to hear about the playground being built in his honor."

She talked a bit about Saul, how he'd always liked children, and about the playground and how she hoped it would look. When she finished the audience clapped.

The principal took the microphone. She gave Joan a hug, which made Joan tense up and step back, then she said, "Thank you so much Joan, for everything."

Joan nodded uncomfortably. "I'm so glad to help," she whispered finally.

The two women stepped off the stage, and the crowd moved to the back table, to the cookies and cake. I tried to find a moment when I could be alone with Joan, to thank her as the principal had asked me to, but it seemed like she was surrounded by a crowd at every possible second. Finally, just as she was leaving, I touched her on the shoulder.

"I want to thank you for the scholarship," I said.

She looked at me blankly.

"Oh right," she smiled broadly. "Of course." She put out her hand to shake mine, and then stooped down to fix the strap of her shoe. "These appearances are murder. They're the absolute worst. I think I'm going to make it a condition that I not appear anywhere I give money. They always want you to appear, though. Why do you think they always want you to appear?"

"I don't know," I said. I nodded as if I understood what she was talking about, as if I, too, were tormented by people who wanted to applaud me and put me up on stage. She held up her hand to wave and then disappeared into the crowd.

The next day, the principal called me to her office.

"Sit," she said when I walked in.

She made me wait in a chair for several minutes while she worked on her computer, then she looked up.

"So, you met Joan Fields?" she asked. She slid her glasses down and gazed at me over them.

"Yes," I said. "I thanked her." I almost added, just like you told me to, but I decided against it.

"I know," she said.

I didn't know how she knew, but I didn't question it. She pushed her glasses back up, and looked down at her computer.

"Joan Fields is an important donor," she said, finally. "It's important that she feel important."

"That's important," I agreed.

"Anyway, I want to let you know, she's chosen you as a mentee. She picks someone every year—generally one of her scholarship students, but not always."

"She picked me?" I asked. "Why?" I couldn't imagine any good reason.

"You must have made a good impression on her," she said. A basketball hit the side of the wall beside the window, and she flinched. "I really should move those courts," she said. "Just get someone to pave them over, move them down."

"What does she do with the person she picks?" I asked.

"Mentors them."

"Oh," I said, "I see." Although really I didn't.

The ball hit the wall again, and she walked over to the window. She opened it, and a blast of hot air wafted in. "Move it on down," she called out. She turned back to me.

"She'd like to take you out to dinner in November. Talk to you a bit about your plans for college. You should bring your parents."

"I have to bring my parents?" I was thinking my mother might be all wrong for the occasion, but she must have misunderstood me because she said:

"Do you not have parents?"

"I do. Kind of. I mean, I have a mom."

"One mom." She put her finger in the air to check something off on an imaginary checklist. "Wonderful. She'll do. Anything else?"

"No," I said.

"Very well then."

I walked out of the office, thinking it over. I hadn't asked for a mentor, but I wasn't necessarily against it. I liked the fact that Joan Fields had chosen me. It didn't matter that I didn't know the criteria.

I walked past the first row of lockers, still thinking about it. Paco was standing at the end, near the water fountain, talking to Sydney. When I passed, he stepped away from her and started to walk with me.

"She hates that you just did that," I told him.

He looked back at Sydney. For a second, we both studied her scowling face, then he said, "Nah, she doesn't care."

"Right," I said. It didn't seem likely to me. "She likes you. I can tell."

Someone jostled me, and I almost dropped my books. For a second, as I shifted to regain them, my elbow brushed his arm.

"She just said pretty much the same thing about you, actually," he said.

I'd been too obvious then. I'd been afraid of that. "That girl," I started, but someone interrupted us. Another girl, a thin, stringy-haired blond, tapped Paco on the shoulder.

"Hey, Fortune," she said to me as an afterthought as she passed. People had been calling me Fortune-Teller, or Fortune for short, ever since Sydney threw the tarot deck at me in class.

She waved in a friendly way and disappeared into the crowd.

"You don't like that name, huh?" Paco said, after she had left.

"You can tell," I said. We were at my locker now. I twirled the combination and opened the door.

"Everyone has a nickname here," he said.

"Nice try," I said.

Emily walked up and he said, "Right, Emily? You probably have a nickname."

"Not me," she said, "but for a while in middle school people called Paco Tight Pants."

"Right," he said. "That's what I'm saying."

"I might try to reinstate that actually," Emily said.

I turned toward Paco. "How did you get it to stop?"

"I bought some different pants."

We all laughed, but really, there isn't anything funny about losing your name.

# TEN

The next day after school, three women showed up at our door. They were dressed similarly, in jeans and plain T-shirts, but one had a saucer-shaped purple hat. None of them were certain they'd come to the right place. I could hear them discussing it through the door.

"Are you sure you wrote the right number down?" the small one said in a large, deep voice. She looked like an ant through the keyhole, but with a large head.

"I'm sure," said the curly-haired, medium-sized one. She had a chime to her voice that reminded me of the spoons my mother hung in a row to catch the wind back home.

"This place has a bad aura," the third one said. This one was taller than the others. She had red hair and broad shoulders, and a tired, loud, no-nonsense voice that made me think of a waitress at a diner. I could picture her serving pancakes, slapping a wet rag around, insulting anyone who deserved it. "No one should live this close to a highway."

"Bad for the soul to be this close to the 405," the curly-haired one agreed.

I felt a little disheartened listening to them. I didn't like the place either, but it didn't mean I liked hearing bad things about it. I opened the door.

"We're looking for Debbie," the short one said. "We work with her at the Tarot Hotline."

My mother had mentioned a group of ladies she talked to sometimes when she went in to get her schedule or pick up her checks.

"Mom!" I called. "Mom!"

A few seconds passed before my mother poked her head out of the bedroom door.

"Where are your manners, Lindsey?" she said. "Let them in."

They didn't wait for me to step back; they just swirled past me. They smelled like wind and dry leaves and something more formal—perfume. It hovered above them in a mixed-up cloud: one part flower, one part citrus, one part musk.

I left them to my mother and walked back to my room, but I had a hard time studying. They laughed too loudly, and they talked too much, and after a while I gave up. I tiptoed past them to the kitchen and opened the refrigerator door.

"Have you gotten the man who purrs like a cat?" the deep-voiced one asked.

"The men are the worst," the one whose voice chimed like a bell replied.

The rest of the women agreed, then the loud one said, "I put my own cat on the phone when Cat Man calls and make myself a snack."

The women laughed like it was all very hysterical, and I shut the refrigerator door. I don't know why the conversation surprised me, but it did. I guess I'd expected the other women at the Tarot Hotline to be real psychics.

I bit into an apple and listened to the women complain some more. They seemed to be having some sort of party, the point of which was to give each other laughable, second-rate things in re-used wrapping paper. I could hear them shrieking when they opened their gifts.

"Lindsey," the loud one said suddenly, "I can see you straight through that wall. Come out and admit you're listening or go about your business."

Her voice startled me. I didn't really think she could see me through the wall, but I backed up a few steps, anyway. "I'm not listening," I said, but I peeked out over the partition anyway.

"Why don't you come out, dear?" the curly-haired one said sweetly. "You know, Maud, it is her home. Sometimes you can be so abrasive."

Maud raised her eyebrows. "You think so?" she asked.

"I do," said curly hair. "I'm Rose, by the way." She pointed at the tiny one with the deep voice, "That's Willow."

I sat down, and Rose patted me on the knee. "It's Willow's birthday," she said. "On our birthdays, we give gifts to everyone so no one feels left out. You have one, too." She handed me a box wrapped in pink paper.

Willow pulled a ribbon off her package and handed it to Maud, who held it up, as if to measure it. She passed it to Rose, who cut it in two and wrapped it in a tight bow.

"What do you think it is?" she asked.

A gust of highway wind blew in the window and swept across the floor. It rustled Maud's hair and lifted the discarded wrappings into the air.

"I don't know," I said.

They laughed.

"Lindsey's a big girl," Rose said. "She knows all about business, don't you now?"

"Yes," I said.

"You just sit here with us and make yourself at home," she said. "You're an honorary South Node Lady now."

The three of them called themselves the South Node Ladies, I soon learned, because their star charts shared a north node moon in Cancer and a south node moon in Capricorn. This meant that their souls' journeys would require them to let go of control, prestige, and materialism (south node characteristics) and move toward emotional sensitivity and nurturing (north node characteristics). The joke they had was that they were above all this. They'd discarded their souls' journeys and relaxed into their south node, where they could be as materialistic as they wanted and do whatever they pleased.

"Lindsey's nodes could be different," Maud said. "We'd have to look it up. But, of course, it's all gobbledygook."

I nodded. I was willing to accept Maud's opinion that it was gobbledygook. Still, I felt strangely honored to be part of their unusual sorority. I leaned back against the wall and waited for Maud to continue.

"Your mother just told us a crazy thing," she said.

It didn't surprise me. "What?" I said.

"She said that you two live off the income from the phone line. You *live* off it!" Willow shrieked.

For the next several minutes, they argued among themselves as to whether they should tell me how they made what they called their "real income." It seemed that they'd decided not to, but then they went ahead and told me anyway. They had a way of talking, one on top of the other, that turned their speech into a collective jumble, but the gist of it was this: The three of them ran a phony spiritualist church for which they solicited donations, mainly from widows, widowers, and people who'd lost loved ones. They called the people they preyed on "marks." They pretended to contact the dead relatives of marks, and then once they won their trust, they asked them to donate large amounts of money to the phony church.

"What do you do with the money then?" I asked. The mechanisms of how scams worked had always interested me, though I'd never much liked carrying them out.

"What do you think, silly?" Rose shouted. "We split it up."

Maud must have thought I was having trouble believing it because she said:

"You see, there's a particular thing about grief that makes people susceptible. They want to believe—will believe, in fact, even if you tell them it's an outright lie. I knew a woman, a pretty good medium, actually, who confessed to the whole thing. Marched right up to the pulpit on a Sunday and told the whole church, every single paying member. We were all concerned, let me tell you, but when the next Sunday rolled around, we had the same kind of crowd. I don't think we lost one member. And the Fox sisters? The founders of Spiritualism? They confessed."

She moved toward me. She was so close now that I could smell the sour, outdoor smell that hung about her clothes. I stared at her eyebrows, the dark, severe arches she must have plucked out and penciled in, and then at the group of tiny red hairs that grew out of the bottom of her chin.

"You should talk in a nicer voice," Rose said. "You'll scare her."

"You should see your face right now," Willow said. "Go look in the mirror, Maud. Go ahead."

Maud waved both comments away. "Did I scare you?" she asked me.

I said no, but in a way, she had. All of them had. The air in the living room just felt different when they were there—electric. I wouldn't call it a premonition, not exactly, but how could I have guessed the extent of the trouble they would bring?

After the women left, I opened my gift—a duck-shaped bumper sticker that said HONK IF YOU BELIEVE IN FATE. I stuck it on our lampshade and walked out to the balcony. Fire season, and the air was thick and hot. The moon was bright red. A striking sight, but it didn't look beautiful to me. The fire in Oregon was still too close. Some of my clothes still smelled of it. I thought of the way a flame looks, orange at the top but blue at the center, and the way the shotgun house had seemed to crouch afterward, to hunker down on itself like a very old man. The way its roof had hung off it on one side like a drooping ear.

The fires that colored the moon tonight were out in Orange County. We weren't in any real danger here, not directly, but a burnt toast, burnt tar smell had traveled as far as our garden, and a heavy gray cloud had settled above us. The ash that fell down from this cloud was as fine and as dry as sifted flour, yet as oily as gasoline. It landed in the pool and floated on the surface, and it clung like glue to the balcony railings. It greased the surface of the outside table and turned it black.

"Hey, Lindsey."

I turned to see Paco. He walked up the balcony, holding the railing, and stopped in front of me. His hair was wet, like he'd just come from the shower, and he smelled like soap and pencil shavings. He was wearing a grocery store uniform: khaki slacks, a white button-down shirt, and a nametag that said ED.

"I didn't know you had a job, Ed."

He looked down at the tag. "I lost mine and the manager said I had to wear one. It's the rule."

"So you stole Ed's?"

"He left it when he quit."

He stepped around my mother's flowerpot and started down the steps. There was something about the quick way he moved away that depressed me, but then, midway down, he stopped and turned.

"Hey," he said. "Do you want to hang out sometime?"

"Sure," I said, very quickly.

He laughed. "Friday?"

"Okay," I tried not to smile in a way that looked over eager, but I'm pretty sure I did.

He left then. I watched him walk out to his car. He kept his shoulders squared and his head up, and he had a kind of skip to his step. After he was gone, I walked down to the garden. I stared at the weeds and the trash that had blown up against the gate, then beyond that, at the highway, at Sepulveda, as its rush hour, parking lot self. I heard a sound like a gunshot—the backfire of a car. Someone cursed and a bottle broke on the street. A blank, black, starless night and the city burned on. I tested the air with my finger and came up with ash.

# ELEVEN

It took me a long time to decide what to wear for the date. My mother had bought a stack of clothes for each of us at a thrift shop in Santa Monica the first week we were in L.A., but I hadn't really looked at them until now. I didn't have high expectations, but when I tried them on, I realized that most of them weren't half bad. Here's some advice: if you are ever in the position where you have to buy all your clothes at thrift shops, do it in Los Angeles. People don't wear their clothes to pieces there. They throw out new things and buy more new things.

I chose the best of the lot, a pair of jeans and a red T-shirt, and fished around in the closet for my shoes. My sneakers didn't look right, and the loafers I wore with my uniform seemed too dowdy, so I borrowed a pair of sandals from my mother's closet. I put on some of her perfume, too, but I immediately regretted it. I smelled like her now, or, to put it another way, I could smell her. I felt like she was in the room with me, and I didn't want her along on the date. Besides, the perfume had a touch of patchouli in it, and I didn't like patchouli. I washed my wrists in the sink to get rid of it, but the patchouli remained. If anything, it deepened. It smelled as though I had a whole row of patchouli candles burning on my skin.

I was still washing the perfume off in the sink when my mother appeared at the bathroom door. "Nice to see you taking some care with your appearance," she said. She looked down at her watch. "Did you say your young man was coming at seven? Because my watch says seven-thirty."

"He said around seven," I said, although he hadn't. He'd said seven. "He probably has some excuse."

"He's five doors down," she said. "What excuse can he have? He got caught in all the traffic of people walking around? What are you doing to your arm? It's all red."

"Nothing," I said. I wiped my arm on the towel. "Do I smell like patchouli to you?"

"Yes. You smell nice. Put a little more on." She picked up the perfume bottle and sprayed it in my direction.

"Don't," I said. "I mean it. Put it down. Maybe I should call him or walk over."

"No!" she said. "That is a thing you must definitely not do." She set the bottle down on the sink and twisted the cap back on.

"No?"

"No. This is what you do. You wait for him to call you. If he did forget, then you act like you forgot, too. Then, if he asks you out again, you turn him down. That's how it works. Trust me on this."

"I think I might call him," I said, but then I heard a knock at the door.

"I'll get it," my mother said.

*I should open it*, I thought. *I should just push past her.* But I didn't. I could discard her advice, but her opinions still lingered. And I still didn't know why he was late. The worry I'd felt just a few minutes earlier over whether he was going to show up had not turned into relief; it had turned into annoyance. Why did he have to be late? Why did he have to set her off like this?

My mother opened the door. "Is someone expecting you?" she asked.

Paco had been leaning on the doorframe when she opened it, but when she spoke, he straightened up. "I think so," he said. "Your daughter is."

She pushed aside an armful of silver bracelets and looked down at her watch. "Hmm," she said. "Well, I don't know about that. She was expecting a young man about an hour ago, but no one showed. Could you be this young man?"

"I am," he said. "I can explain."

My mother frowned. "No need for that. She's gone out already, with a different young man."

"I don't want to contradict you, ma'am," he said. "But I see her. She's right behind you."

I stepped toward the door. I was ready to talk to him and hear his excuse, but my mother was too quick. She slammed the door shut and thrust the bolt down.

"Well that takes care of that," she said. She slapped her hands together and turned toward the kitchen.

"Why did you do that?" I asked. She'd gone too far, now. "I want to go out with him, did you forget that part?" I lifted a rung of the Venetian blind and peered out. If he was still there, I might go out and see what he had to say.

I spotted him by the railing, tugging at the wisteria vine. It was a strong vine, hard to cut, even with scissors, but he managed to rip off a piece. He bunched it up into something that looked a little bit like a bouquet, and knocked at the door again.

My mother opened the door. "She doesn't want any flowers," she said. "She sees right through that kind of thing."

"I didn't think she did," he said. "I brought these for you." He plucked one flower out of the bunch and handed it to my mother.

My mother tried to look stern, but the sides of her lips quivered. Her frown turned up at the edges. She liked flowers, and she liked getting them. I don't think she realized they were from her very own vine.

"It's rare to meet such a caring and involved mother," he said.

"Uh huh," she said. She frowned, again, to let him know she wasn't completely buying it, but she let him in. "A second chance is only as good as what you make it, young man." She disappeared into the kitchen to find a vase.

We walked out the door, and Paco explained that the reason he was late had to do with his car.

"I've been trying for an hour to get my father to let me take the car tonight. He thinks I dinged up the door."

"Did you?"

He waved off the question. We walked past his window and three little faces leaned out. The tallest one, a girl of about eight or nine years old, shouted, "No car, Paco! No way!" She ducked back inside, behind the curtain, and disappeared in a sea of giggles.

"That's how he said it," Paco explained, "Just like that. No car, no way! It's all the English he knows. He got to use all of his words today. It was a great day for him. . . . I see you, Gabby. Go away."

More giggles. "Are you going to kiss her, Paco?" Gabby called out after us as we walked away.

"I might," he called back to her. Then to me, he said, "That's Gabby. She's a real pain." After a while, he added, "She's my favorite sister."

I nodded. The inner workings of a family had always interested me, but I didn't feel like I knew enough about it to comment.

"She's the reason my lunches are so bad," he went on. "She steals all the good stuff before I go to school. It's pretty funny, actually. You should see it. She takes it behind the couch with her and gets all crouched down, thinking she's hiding it. If I say, 'What you got there, Gabby?' know what she says? 'Nothing you got to know about, Paco. Nothing you got to know.'"

It sounded kind of bratty to me, but he laughed. It really broke him up. "Nothing you got to know," he repeated.

We walked out to the road in front of the building and stood beside the curb. I could feel the wind from each car as it passed. Paco leaned up against a telephone pole and looked up at the sky. I wanted him to stand closer. I wanted him to go away, too, so I could organize my thoughts about him.

"Well, where do you want to go?" I asked, finally.

He shrugged. "Just walk, I guess," he said.

I don't think either of us knew we were going to the school until we got there. We sat down in the playground at the elementary building, on top of the old merry-go-round, and I studied his profile in the dark.

"Where'd you say you were from again?" he asked.

"New Hampshire."

"You kind of talk like someone from Oregon."

"Oregon?"

"Yeah, like that. You just said Or-e-gun. People from Oregon always say it that way."

"I'm not from Oregon," I snapped.

"Okay," he said. "What's it like out there, out in New Hampshire?"

"You know," I said, "same as everywhere." Why did he have to play twenty questions?

"Everywhere isn't the same."

"It had mountains," I said. "It was pretty. Okay?" I had no idea what New Hampshire looked like. I didn't know why he was so interested all of a sudden in New Hampshire.

We didn't say anything for a while. I guess we were both trying to figure out why his questions had annoyed me so much. He spun the merry-go-round around slowly, dragging his foot, and the stars swirled by in bright lines.

"Did you hear about the playground?" Paco said.

"No. What?"

"The contractor substituted the wood with some cheap stuff with a ton of arsenic in it. They're going to have to rip out the whole thing and start again."

I stopped the merry-go-round with my foot. "Where'd you hear that?" I hadn't heard any announcement about it at the school.

"I'm kind of on the committee. I'm the head, actually. The thing is, we don't want to ask the donor for more money."

"Joan Fields," I told him. Our scholarship sponsor. My mentor.

"Right. We don't want to say, hey, we botched it up. Can you give us some more?"

"So what will you do?"

He shrugged. "We're thinking of doing this carnival fundraiser thing at the school." He took a pen light out of his pocket and aimed it under the floor of the merry-go-round. "Look under," he said.

"What's there?" I wasn't sure I wanted to crawl down on the ground.

"Go ahead, you'll see."

I looked. Someone had drawn a circle in bright blue pen. Inside it they'd written EMILY, SCOTT, PACO in all caps, in a giant childish hand.

"You were all always together, huh?"

"It was the scholarship thing. People picked on us."

"I don't think people really alienate you guys all that much anymore," I said. Girls were always waving to Paco. "Not as much as you guys think, anyway." It was my opinion that they had sectioned themselves off to some degree.

"Maybe not," he said, considering it. He looked over at the building. "We used to stand over there at recess." He pointed at the side of the steps. "The other kids would bring out these stacks of Pokémon cards, just stacks and stacks of them. We never had any. We'd just stand around bouncing the same stupid ball off the wall."

I could see it as he talked. The three of them, shorter, but looking pretty much the same, bouncing the ball. I wondered where Sydney was in all of it. I imagined her with two blond pigtails, sitting on the bottom step with a big stack of Pokémon cards.

"I remember those cards," I said. "I didn't have any either. My mother said I should play with tarot cards instead."

"I guess it's pretty much the same."

"It's not," I said.

"You know, I don't think kids play with them as much anymore."

"Tarot cards?"

"No, Pokémon cards. When I got my first paycheck at the grocery store, I bought Gabby a whole stack of those cards. All the really good ones. You know what she said to me? 'Buy me something else, Paco. I don't like these.' You know, it'll probably be like that with the playground. I'll want my sisters to have it, but in the end when it's built, they probably won't care."

"It's still nice," I said. "It's a nice thing to do."

"Well, I'm a nice person," he agreed. He pointed at the sky, and his hand brushed against the back of mine. For a second, he was close enough, almost, to kiss me, but then he said, "Look at the moon."

I turned my head cautiously. I had been trying not to look at the moon all night. It was a waning moon, which meant it was a bad time to begin new things.

"It doesn't mean anything," I said, more to myself than to him.

"Why would the moon mean something?" he said.

"That's what I just said. It doesn't."

"It's something people talk about in Oregon, huh?"

I let the comment about Oregon go. The interested way he was looking at me made me nervous. Up until now, no one had cared enough to scrutinize my story.

We stood up and started back to the street. We crossed the road and wound around and up a hill, through a neighborhood of large, brightly lit houses. This was where the rich people lived. If anyone lived here at all. I'd never once seen anyone on the street.

"See that house," I told Paco. I pointed at the white columned house on the corner. My mother and I had talked about living there, one day, when the psychic reading business took off. "I'm going to live there."

"Yeah?"

"It could happen," I said. I stopped on the sidewalk in front of it. Really, there was something sad about that house. It always looked empty. I wanted it anyway.

We looped down the hill and back toward the Sepulveda complex. I saw its windows first, the small bright squares of light flung open to the night air. Then I heard the familiar mix of radio stations, voices, and languages that always rose up. The long-faced man who played the hubcap in the courtyard said, "For the lovebirds," and rapped out a high tin beat. For one dizzy second, Paco spun me around, but then the music stopped and the drummer bent down to root around in the trash.

When the dance ended, we didn't drop our hands right away. Paco took a step toward me. I think he meant to kiss me, but the upstairs window to my apartment opened. The Christmas lights went on, the ones my mother displayed year-round on our door and railing, and they lit up the spot where we stood like stage lights. I looked up. I could feel my mother's eyes on me. But where was she watching from? The kitchen window? The porch light made a buzzing sound above my left ear.

Paco took a step back. "See you at school," he said.

Later, after he'd left, I stood in the dark living room, listening to my mother pretend to snore and thinking about those words: *See you in school.* It was the kind of thing, I decided, that a person might say to just about anyone. It didn't seem promising . . . at all. I worried about it, but then my phone lit up and I saw his text message: "Night."

"Night," I typed back.

I brought the phone into my room in case he texted again, but he didn't. After a while, I fell asleep with it in my hand.

# TWELVE

Paco and I were spending more and more time together. I didn't plan these meetings; I didn't have to. Paco just appeared. I'd cross the courtyard to the laundry room, a basket in my hands, and suddenly he'd fall into step beside me. Or I'd walk down the hallway at school and find him at my locker, leaning against it, waiting for me.

We generally went to Paco's place after school. There was more noise there, and more snacks, and what seemed like a dozen children underfoot, but sometimes we went to mine. He liked the quiet, he said. He liked the way my mother retreated into her room and left us alone. She and Paco had developed a way of dealing with each other, a relationship based on polite watchfulness and careful avoidance on both parts.

It bothered me, at first, that my mother didn't like him, but then I came to the realization that this was actually a good sign. She didn't have the best judgment when it came to men. I only had to do a quick review of her dating history to assure myself of that.

First, there was Tom. He had knocked on our door one night wearing cowboy boots and a tall black hat and had whisked her away to a country-dancing establishment.

She'd had a good time. She danced with every man in the place except Tom. She left him at the bar, drinking alone, until she got him into a fight over a comment she made about somebody's hat. We never saw Tom again.

Brian came next. Big Brian with his new Trans Am. He'd bought the car earlier, the very same day as their date, and he offered to let her drive it. He must not have known she wasn't a good driver, but he found out pretty quickly when she crashed the car into a concrete pole in a parking garage.

She'd had no other dates that I'd known about, unless you considered her husband, my father, a man who had died sixteen years ago.

"Why does she always look at me like that?" Paco asked one afternoon.

"It's something she does to everyone."

He shifted on the steps. We watched the bees buzz around in the rose bush at the center of the courtyard, until he said, "That crystal ball thing she has is weird."

And then I understood: Paco was frightened of my mother. "The ball in the dragon claw? If your throat feels tight, like it's got peanut butter in it, tell me. Okay?"

"What?" he said. For a second, he looked alarmed, but then he shrugged it off. "Hey, I have a question for you. Do you think she, or maybe you, could contact my brother for me? He's, what's the term you guys use? On the other side."

"I'm sorry," I said. It was a grown-up, awkward thing to say, but I couldn't think of anything better.

He nodded. "It was a drive-by shooting. He was just in the wrong place."

"Was it here? On Sepulveda?"

He leaned back, into the slanted shade from the roof. "No. We moved after. My mom got this idea in her head that I would get shot, too. Or join some gang. I was like, seven, but she worries ahead like that. She went down to the church, talked to the priest."

"And got you the scholarship," I finished.

I tried to imagine Paco in a rough neighborhood, on a precarious street. It seemed to me he might not last all that long in the type of situation where he had to keep his wits about him. He was strong, physically, but he didn't always pay attention to things. Just that morning, he'd stepped in dog poop and left a trail of it through the hallway of the school.

"I was standing next to him when he died. On the same sidewalk. He got shot. I didn't." He paused. "It's why I have to do something great. Build, like, a hundred play-grounds for kids or something." He looked down at the ground and laughed.

I had the sudden urge to tell him about my own childhood. Oregon. The way it felt like the ground was shaking the day we drove away. The way the whole world felt tipped every time I found out my mother had lied to me again. I guess I just wanted him to know me the way I was starting to know him. In the car, she'd said we'd have to tell a few lies about ourselves—where we were from, things like that—but I hadn't realized, when I'd agreed to it, how hard it would be.

"So can you guys contact him?" Paco said.

"Your brother?"

He nodded.

It took me a second to figure out what to say. "I'd like to," I said.

"But you won't."

I shook my head.

"Why not?"

*Because it would be a great big lie*, I thought, but I said, "Well, there are a lot of reasons. We're not mediums, for one. We don't contact the dead."

I wanted to tell him the truth, but he'd just said all that stuff about changing the world. How could I admit the thing I did to change the world was scam people?

"Plus, it's important that I keep my work separate," I said. "There are all these things I have to do before I read for people. It works better if I don't know the person too well."

"Like what?" he said.

"Well, I have to bring up this wall of protective white light, and I have to ground myself." This part was true.

He looked amused now. "And you ground yourself how?"

"By keeping one foot on the ground at all times." It sounded stupid, now that I'd said it aloud. "I didn't make it up. I read it in a book." How could I explain the way it felt to sit in a room with people sometimes? The heavy way their problems could weigh on you, sucking you down.

"Hmm," he said, leaning over me. My flip-flop slipped through one of the rungs of the steps and fell to the patio below. "Are you grounded now?" he asked.

I couldn't answer because, now, we were kissing. I put my arms around his neck and curled my big toe around the metal rung of the step.

"Being grounded is overrated," I said.

Paco and I didn't tell Emily and Scott about us until we had been together for two weeks. It wasn't that we were trying to keep it a secret. It just didn't come up. Then, one day at lunch, Emily caught on. We were leaning against each other, laughing at something, when she said, "You two need to get together."

We must have looked at each other in a suspicious way because she said, "Well, finally."

Scott looked up. "I knew about it," he said.

We all turned to look at him. He spoke so infrequently that, when he did, it generally carried some weight. "I saw them holding hands in the hall."

"Well, call me the last to know," Emily said.

"Sorry," I said. It seemed like I should apologize. I didn't know why.

"Well, that's great," Emily said. "I finally get a friend. A girl friend. No offense, Scott. No offense, Paco, but I finally get a friend that's a girl, and this happens?"

"What happens?" I asked.

"Paco ruins it again." She picked the Twinkie out of Scott's lunch, split it in three pieces, and gave one to everyone but Paco.

"I didn't ruin anything," Paco said.

"Tell her about Sydney, Paco."

"Emily has a stupid grudge against me about Sydney not being her friend anymore or something."

I was surprised. I wouldn't have thought she'd be the type to be friends with Sydney, ever, but I could see from the way she crossed her arms and glared at Paco that it was true.

"It's not stupid, Paco," she said.

"It is stupid," Paco said.

"Here's what will happen," Emily said. "You guys will be together for a week, maybe two. Then Paco will do his thing and move on. He'll get sick of you, just like he got sick of Sydney. You'll get all mad about it and you won't sit with us anymore."

"Is that what you do?" I asked Paco. "Is that your thing?" I was a little worried. Emily knew him better than I did; I'd seen their ancient circle of names beneath the merry-go-round.

"No," Paco said. "Tell her, Scott."

Scott didn't say anything.

"Thanks, man." Paco shook his head.

Scott took a bite of his sandwich. He slid his glasses up a bit on his nose, and said, "He's different around you. I'd go as far as to say I've never seen him so into anyone. You'll dump him. That's my opinion."

It was more than I'd ever heard Scott say, except maybe about the science fair.

"Thanks," Paco said, again. "I think."

Emily stood. She was really getting angry now. She stomped around, grabbing up everyone's lunch, even the stuff we hadn't eaten, and threw it all in the trashcan in one giant heap.

"I was eating that," Scott said.

"Don't get it out of the trash," Paco said. "Don't go there, man."

I stood and walked past Scott, over to Emily, and hugged her. She'd surprised me. I hadn't known she'd cared that much about whether I sat with her.

"I'll still sit with you guys," I said, "Even if he dumps me. Because what other friends do I have?"

She laughed, but she still looked unsure.

"You're my best friend here." As soon as I said it, I knew it was true. We'd grown close over the past few months. "And I'll never go back to Oregon, or see anyone from there, so I guess you're my best friend out of everywhere."

"Oregon!" Paco jumped up. "I knew it. Why in the world did you say you were from New Hampshire?"

I wanted to shoot myself in the mouth. What had I done? I scrambled to come up with an excuse.

"I don't know," I said. "It seemed cooler, I guess."

"It's not," Emily said. "New Hampshire? It's not."

The three of them looked at me as though I'd lost my mind.

# THIRTEEN

November arrived, and with it the night of my scheduled dinner with my mentor. Joan sent me an email telling me to pick a place, so I picked The Lobster in Santa Monica. It was the only restaurant on our List of Things for a Better Life, and I wanted to cross off an item. While my mother bumped around in the bathroom fixing her hair, I looked everywhere for that list. I found it, finally, in my mother's purse, shoved into an old powder compact and folded into a triangle. One day, when I'd been in a particularly bad mood, I'd scribbled A List of Ways to Get Away from my Mother on the back of it. The ideas I came up with were: take the Big Blue Santa Monica Bus to any stop and get off, fake my own death, and leave for college.

My mother must have seen this list because in the margins, in red pen, she had written, THE LAST ONE IS YOUR BEST BET. I turned the list over. She'd written on the List of Things for a Better Life list, too. It had more items now, although lines 21 through 30 all said the same thing: COLLEGE FOR LINDSEY! COLLEGE FOR LINDSEY! COLLEGE FOR LINDSEY! The last item, number 31, said, A BETTER LIFE FOR LINDSEY.

I stared at my mother's bubbly handwriting. It looked so upturned and hopeful, so fat with goodwill, that I couldn't help but smile. I crossed off The Lobster with a quick slash of my pen. Then I folded it again and put it back into the compact.

The Lobster was a large glass and concrete building at the foot of the Santa Monica pier. It looked very elegant, but at the same time, a bit out of place, like a woman in a cocktail dress showing up for a carnival. Beside and behind the restaurant, the pier was in full swing. People of all shapes, ages, and sizes walked up and down the weathered planks, shoulder to shoulder, or screamed in the air from various rides. The Ferris Wheel appeared twice—once in the air, above all the chaos, and once below it—as a splatter of lights on black water.

When my mother stepped onto the pier, the crowd stepped back to let her pass. She had a shimmery gold dress on, and it looked good on her. It's hard to explain, but there is a certain kind of glamour that hangs about my mother that can, at times, seem almost like magic. If you look closely at her, it's easy to see that she's not completely, perfectly beautiful. Her face is too round, her lips are thin, her nose upturns. Her bottom front teeth are slightly crooked. For a good part of her life, she was more than a little bit overweight, but even then most people didn't notice. It has to do, I suppose, with the way she carries herself or else with the way she sees herself. It's her height or her hair or her smile or her voice. I don't know what it is, but I do know this: whatever it is, I don't have it.

I walked a step behind my mother, clomping up to the restaurant in my too-big thrift store boots. I was thin enough, but too angular. Pants were too long or too short. Sleeves hung from my shoulders in a floppy, baggy way. I'd gotten better about it, but still, most of the time, I couldn't face the confusion of clothes. I'd put my school uniform on, even on weekends, or I'd resort to my old pile of black T-shirts.

Joan was waiting beside the door, dressed in a light green pantsuit that made her look like a grasshopper. Her hair, straight at the assembly, curled tonight into tight ringlets around her face. She greeted us and said, "Good choice. Saul and I never came here."

"Saul?" my mother asked.

"My late husband."

My mother touched her arm. "I'm sorry."

Joan nodded.

We followed the hostess, a slim girl with short, white-blond hair, to the far edge of the room where a small square table stood in front of a glass wall. At sunset, this seat must have made for a great view, but it was too dark now to see much of anything. I peered out of it anyway and faced myself: me turned toward me, dressed all wrong and looking sullen, beside the upright, open menus of the others. Behind me, the waitstaff darted about, crossing the room in all directions, like fish in a bowl.

After the waiter took our order, we were quiet for a few seconds. The principal had suggested I ask Joan about her career as a real estate investor if there was a lull in conversation, but I wasn't particularly interested in real estate. I was just about to ask her anyway when she said, "I have something to give you."

I looked over at my mother. We hadn't known that Joan would bring a gift.

My mother cleared her throat. "We have a present for you, too, Joan. We'd give it to you right now, but we forgot it at home."

"The mentee never gives the mentor a present," Joan explained.

"Of course," my mother said. She laughed, a little too loudly. It was something she did, sometimes, with people who had gone to college. That, or she'd make up a college she'd supposedly gone to and say stupid things about it. "I was joking."

"I don't care about presents, anyway," Joan said. "I'd rather give them. Go ahead and open it, Lindsey." She handed me a flat package in silver paper and looked at me in an eager way until I opened it. When I did, a book fell out.

I turned the book over in my hand and read the title aloud, "*College Bound: A Handbook for Your First Year.*"

"Thanks," I said.

Joan clapped her hands together. "Good. I was worried you wouldn't accept it."

I couldn't think of any way I could have given Joan the impression that I would ever *not* accept just about anything, but I nodded anyway. "Thanks," I said again.

Joan leaned forward. She picked her napkin up and placed it on her lap. "Anyway, I want to let you know I'm here for you. If you have questions about college. Anything. Just let me know. Have you finished filling out your applications?"

"Almost," I said. Applications were due at the end of the month. I'd hoped to be finished by now, but the process hadn't gone as quickly as I'd thought.

"We were kind of thinking of making a college visit," my mother said. "With our finances, though, we may not be able to afford it."

We'd never talked about any college visits. If we had, we could easily have gone. The college I wanted most was only a few hours away. I glared at her across the table.

"I might be able to help finance a trip," Joan said, taking the bait. "Where would you go?"

"UCSC," I said.

"Or somewhere farther," my mother said. "Weren't you talking about something out east, Lindsey? Something you needed a plane ticket for?"

She was really starting to irritate me. I truly wished she would just shut up. "I like UCSC," I said. "It has the astronomy program I want."

"Maybe one of your backup schools," my mother said.

"My backup schools are in California, too," I said.

My mother frowned and stabbed her bread with her knife. I knew what she was thinking. She didn't really care about the school visits. The reason she was angry was that I refused to talk about college with her, but I was talking about it now with Joan. I'd hurt her feelings, but I wasn't sure I cared at that moment.

"The one thing that bothers me about astronomy," Joan said, randomly, "is Pluto. Poor, little, demoted-from-planet Pluto."

I nodded. It did seem sad. "I like the moon," I offered.

Joan looked up as if she could see the moon in the ceiling of the restaurant. "Ah, the moon," she said. "There is something very permanent about it. Don't you think?"

I didn't know what she was getting at exactly. "I guess so."

"There's no erosion on the moon. No wind. No water. Did you know that the footsteps the astronauts made in 1969 are still there?"

I did, but I'd never really thought about it. I considered the moon the way she saw it: a dustless, cautious place where emptiness ruled and footprints were as permanent as scars. "I think it's more the far-away nature of it," I said finally, "that appeals to me."

My mother must have felt like she had been quiet too long, because she said, "Have either of you ever played that card game? Where you shoot the moon?"

Joan and I both looked at her.

"I keep getting this feeling like I'm sitting across from myself thirty years ago." Joan motioned to me. "We're so much alike."

I nodded. It hadn't occurred to me, but I wasn't necessarily against it.

"Don't you think, Debbie?" she asked my mother. "Don't you think Lindsey and I are alike?"

My mother looked back and forth between us. She must have been as confused as I was as to what we had in common. "Only time will tell," she said.

Joan nodded. "Excuse me while I find the restroom. I wonder where it is?"

Joan left to circle the restaurant, looking for the restroom in every corner, and my mother picked another roll out of the breadbasket. She took a small bite and set it down. By now, she'd stacked up a small hill of sampled, discarded bread.

"You should think more carefully about who you look up to," she said.

"What are you talking about?" I asked. I didn't know why she couldn't just let me enjoy the attention.

She rolled her eyes. "Oh, Joan, I'd love to go to UCSC! Oh, Joan, let's talk about the moon. It's so far away. So permanent!"

"Stop it," I said. "Just stop."

She picked up her drink and dumped it in the flower vase in the center of the table. "Okay. But it is kind of silly the way you look up to her."

"Who should I look up to then?" I asked.

She looked surprised. "Well, how about me? You could start with me."

I laughed, but almost instantly regretted it. It was a mean, bitter laugh, and it sounded bad, even to my ears. Besides, I did look up to her. She'd had her influence, good and bad. There wasn't any way I could deny that.

We didn't stay very long after that. Joan must have noticed the mood just wasn't as good anymore because after a while she said that she'd get in touch with me. She wished me luck, and we all walked outside to the pier.

"My driver will take you home," Joan said. "I'm going to walk on the beach."

"By yourself?" my mother said. "We'll come with you."

Somewhere, below us on the beach, a man hooted. A bottle broke in the dark.

"Don't be silly," Joan said.

There didn't seem to be anything we could do but go, so we climbed in the limo. Before we drove off, I rolled down the window and waved to Joan. She looked back, not seeing me, before she turned to face the black water.

"She's going to get mugged in about two minutes," my mother said.

I rolled up my window and leaned back in my seat. "Well, the fish was good," I said.

"You thought so? Hey, do you think I need to tip the driver?"

I fiddled with the television, then opened a drawer full of mini bags of chips. I stuffed them into my purse and said, "I have no idea."

"Well, I don't have any cash."

"Then no," I said.

The driver must have expected something, though, because he waited a few seconds before stepping back into the car. After he drove off, we started up the path to the apartment.

"It's funny, don't you think, her being a widow?" my mother asked.

*Why would that be funny?* I wondered, but then something clicked. I remembered the South Node Ladies, the crazy loud bunch from the Tarot Hotline who had gathered in our living room.

"Oh no," I said. "You can't have her."

She paused, thoughtfully. "You have to admit, she does fit the profile."

"I don't believe this," I said. "You're trying to steal my mentor."

A light went on in the apartment across the way. "Keep your voice down," she said. She put her hand on the doorknob and stopped. "I'm not going to steal anybody," she said.

We didn't talk about Joan again for some time. I finished my college applications and sent them off, and my mother busied herself with the phone line. December arrived. Christmas wreaths popped up on the doors, and Santa appeared in shorts on the street. We set up a cheap tree, and hung some tinsel on our balcony, and my mother strung lights around the couch and up the wall.

I did my Christmas shopping at the Santa Monica thrift shop. I bought my mother an aloe plant, Emily a book, and Paco a sweater. My mother gave me some clothes and a heart-shaped box, and Paco gave me a moonstone necklace. The stone was oval, pale orange, smooth to the touch and bright with reflected light. The second I saw it I felt bad about the sweater.

"I love the sweater," he said, but the more I looked at him in it, the more I noticed the sleeves were too long. I wore the moonstone necklace constantly, even to sleep.

During all of the festivities, I must have forgotten to watch my mother carefully, because not long after Christmas, I overheard her on the phone with Joan. When I confronted her, she claimed she had been thanking her for the holiday candies Joan had sent, but the chummy way they had been talking made me think they'd spoken a few times before.

She was laying the groundwork. I was sure of it. But was she working on her own? I began to find clues: coffee cups, slips of wrapping paper, odd bumper stickers. I'd catch my mother looking at me in the hallway, out of the corner of her eye, and I'd get the sense that she was waiting, that she and the others were circling me. She had an outdoor smell about her now. As if she'd been running with a pack of wolves.

I walked down to the courtyard and propped my Moon Sign notebook on top of a plastic reindeer. The moon was heavy, low and full. Large enough to howl at, but it had a blurry, wet storm ring around it.

*It doesn't rain in Southern California,* I wrote. *This moon is a liar.*

But just before I went inside, I felt the first drops.

# FOURTEEN

The Sepulveda apartments weren't made for rain. The first day it rained, our ceiling turned dark, and the second day, it sagged. The third day, the rain came through. We pulled pots and pans out of damp cupboards and set them down to gather what they could. The water we collected was cloudy and rust-colored and it smelled like tin. Sediment swirled on the surface and sank to the bottom, but the part in the middle was clear. You could drink it if you had to, if you were desperate enough. It probably was what we had been drinking.

In the morning, my mother called the manager and that evening he arrived wearing low-slung jeans and a low-slung tool belt and carrying a hammer. He stood at the door and pulled at his mustache as he took it all in: the slippery floors, the various holes, the water-swirled smelly furniture, our sunken posture, and my mother's sullen face.

"Can't do much about it," he said. He waved his arm in a giant semicircle, a gesture, I suppose, that meant *everything*. "I could call someone about the roof, but it doesn't make sense. You're in L.A. now; you've got to remember that. It'll dry up, and it won't rain again for months. I tell everyone the same thing. Just wait and it will go away. Now, the woman two doors down has a leak right above her bed. You should have heard the way she carried on about it. I told her, just move the bed, lady. Use some sense for once in your life and move the bed."

He left without offering any further assistance or advice, but he did leave us some large plastic buckets. At first glance these seemed better than the pots and pans— they were bigger and could hold more water—but in the end, they grew too heavy to empty. It took both of us to push them out the door and kick them over. When we finished, we both stood still for a moment, listening to the slow thump of rain against hollow plastic.

"You heard what the man said," my mother told me. "It'll dry up. The problem will be solved."

"But maybe not the smell," I said.

"Maybe not," she said thoughtfully.

We sat down to dinner: a can of tuna fish split between us and the last half of a package of saltine crackers. Then we pushed the TV to the back of the room to keep it dry and watched it late into the night. My mother brought out her old Miss America Pageant videos, the one of her competing on TV and the others, the home videos. She popped in one of the homemade ones and we sat down on the couch to watch it.

The makeup scenes came first. How much is too much? My mother and her sister disagreed. Then the practice shots, my mother with a book on her head. "Straighter," her sister said. "Look tall." Then the arrival in Atlantic City. Storefronts and casinos and the Atlantic Ocean, followed by an unsteady shot of my mother alone, belting out a pretty decent harmonica on States Avenue, two days and counting until the show. There was nothing of the show itself. That was on the other video, the professional one, recorded from live TV. This video skipped over the show and to the end. To after the end, actually, to my mother and her sister hugging each other and stumbling to the car. They were crying the loud, dramatic sobs of bad actresses, but when the camera zoomed in, I could see it was real. My mother had her hair pulled up and off her face in a high ponytail, and her face was scrubbed raw. She looked painfully young, even to me. The dream was over. That much was certain. What would she do with the rest of her life?

My mother shifted on the couch. A tear welled up in one eye, and she wiped it away with the back of her fist. Even now, the video had the power to disturb her. "I wanted it so much. And I was pretty thin actually, but I guess it was the ten pounds. Everyone said it was. Our lives would have been different, you know, if I hadn't gained that weight."

I didn't have to concentrate to do the math to know I was born just six months after the pageant. That it was me who had made her gain the weight. It was me who had ruined it. It was on the tip of my tongue to apologize, to beg for forgiveness and to promise I would never spoil anything for her ever again, but something in my heart stayed hard.

"You said you didn't lose the pageant because of me," I said.

She turned off the TV, and without the friendly sound of it, the darkness seemed to move in. It swirled around us like a palpable thing, and I pulled the afghan closer. Outside, the rain made a tapping sound on the metal steps.

"This thing with Joan," she said. "We could do it."

"It's not right," I said. Making up someone's future was one thing, but pretending to speak to the dead? And cheating a widow?

She adjusted the video and turned it back on. I looked up at the screen, at her young face, crying, and I could feel it, too. I felt it even more, probably, because I knew what was ahead for her. *She didn't ask for a child*, I thought. *She probably didn't want one at all.*

"I'd give it back to you if I could," I said, and I meant it. I wished I could rewind the show and watch her hurry up the steps backward to take the crown.

She turned back to the screen, and I walked out the door.

I ducked under the sheet of water that fell from the roof like a blurred window and made my way down the steps.

My mother could be right about the scam, I thought. Joan had a lot of money. Maybe even enough to go around. But even if she did, even if I took the whole question of the money out of it, I still had Saul to consider. Because how would Saul feel about it? Receiving messages from the dead is a tricky thing, if the dead don't really send them. No one likes to be misquoted, and the dead can be slandered like anyone else. It's a type of identity theft, if you think about it. Only what you are stealing is not credit, not a name, but something much harder to define: the exact, untainted memory of the deceased.

"I'm not a thief," I said aloud, but the rain snatched my voice away. I wasn't sure I believed it anyway.

A light came on across the complex, in Paco's room, and it struck me suddenly how little any of us really know each other. How little we might like each other if we did. A second passed and his window opened. He leaned his head out and said, "That you, Lindsey? Out in the rain?"

"It's me." I walked up the steps and stood outside his window.

"You're all wet."

I looked down at myself. "I am."

He laughed. "Hold on a second." He swung himself out through the window, over the top in one fluid motion. His shoe scraped the sill just before he landed beside me.

"What happened?" he asked.

I leaned up against his chest and listened to his heartbeat. My hair left a wet mark on his shirt when I pulled away.

"I kind of had a fight with my mother," I said.

He pushed my wet hair behind my ear. "About what?"

"It's complicated," I said.

He put his hand on my arm, on the part where the shirt stopped and my shoulder began, and leaned in to kiss me. His mouth was warm in the rain. I took a step back, and my right foot landed in a puddle.

As if on cue, the sound of his mother calling him carried through the open window to us. "Paco!" she called. "Dónde estás?"

"Shh." Paco said. "Ignore it."

We listened to his mother move around inside the apartment, her voice and her steps growing louder and more frequent and more and more angry until finally he gave up and went in. After he left, I looked up at my own window. My mother's head was framed, centered like a photograph, but bobbing back and forth. She was looking for me. Rain clung to the porch light and pooled in bright dots on the window.

She didn't ask for me, I thought, or probably want me very much, but she does love me now. I knew that for certain. I was almost to the top of the steps when the door swung open.

"You're soaked," she said. She put her jacket on top of me and wrapped it tight.

"This thing," I said, "about Joan."

"You're still thinking about that?" She opened the door. Warm air and the smell of coffee hit me in the face.

"You're thinking about it, too."

She shook her head. "When things get bad enough, you'll see it. You'll come around."

It didn't take very long for things to get bad enough for me to see what she was talking about. The very next day at lunch, when I sat down with the others, I didn't have a bag to add to the pile.

"You eat first, then," Emily said. "That's how it works."

They watched me in a worried way, throwing the kind of glances at each other that let me know they'd discussed me.

"I was running late," I said. "I forgot to pack it. That's all."

It was partly true. I had been running late. True, too, that the fridge had been empty. We hadn't gotten the check from the phone line yet, which meant we hadn't gone to the store. A rolling blackout had caused my mother, just the other night, to discard a perfectly good chunk of cheese I might have made into a sandwich. In other words, a great variety of temporary factors would eventually work themselves out, but there was no telling that to any of them.

"It's happened to all of us," Emily said. "Why do you think we do it?"

I didn't really think that it had, but I was too hungry to care. I ate half of Emily's ham sandwich and drank all of Scott's chocolate milk before I looked up.

While the others pretended to talk about other things, I looked behind them at the fountain. I watched the water bubble up between the shell-shaped stones and remembered the rain and the videos we'd watched the night before. Suddenly, the thing with Joan didn't seem as bad as it once had, and I knew that I had made a decision.

The things we do define us. They become us eventually, but I guess I thought I could let go of it in the end. Next year, when I left, I'd leave this behind, too. I didn't really believe it, though. I knew time didn't really change things, that it only dulled them. And I knew I'd never been good at letting things go.

# FIFTEEN

We began the scam with something called a grocery swap. My mother refused to tell me what it was or how we would do it, which worried me some, but not enough to press her for more information. She was generally secretive, and only occasionally dangerously secretive. Still, it irritated me.

When we pulled up to Joan's house, I said, "I don't know why you have to be so dramatic about everything."

She ignored me and pointed up at the house. "Take a look at that."

The house itself didn't surprise me. It looked pretty much the same as it had in the picture we found on the Internet. Huge and box-shaped, the faded green color of old money, it had a long curved driveway that stretched out in front of it like a wide tongue. It had a gray tile roof, a large white door, an ornate, flower-covered balcony, and a long row of windows that faced seaward, bright with reflected sun. We parked just below the driveway, next to a blue car at the side of the road, and did our best to look inconspicuous.

"Do you think it's tipping to the side?" my mother asked. She cocked her head sideways and leaned out the car window.

121

I did the same thing. "Yes."

"It looks like it could just topple to the sea."

I pictured the house falling from its perch, rolling top-over-bottom down the hill and over the highway, all the way to the ocean, splitting open like an egg. There was something forlorn about it, and not just because it was leaning to one side. The lawn was cut short, the garden was tended, the sprinklers were going at a hundred miles an hour. But for some reason, I couldn't help but get the feeling that it was vacant. It may have been the curtains, the way they were drawn, every one of them against the sun, or it may have been the group of seagulls that had settled on the roof. A newspaper flew past us and flapped down the cliff to the ocean.

"What comes next?" I asked.

"We wait for her grocery delivery. She said on the phone the truck comes between one and three o'clock."

"It could come at three o'clock?" I said. It was only one. That was two full hours away. I couldn't believe it.

"Maybe," she said. "But it's kind of nice, don't you think, sitting here? We don't get the chance to talk much anymore."

"We don't?" I said.

She shook her head.

"Okay," I said. "What do you want to talk about?"

"How about your name?"

"My name?"

She nodded as if I'd confirmed something. "Your father picked it."

"He did?" I said. I liked that. He'd died when I was a baby, but I liked to feel he'd had some small part in my life.

Even if it was just to give me my name. "What did you want to name me?"

"Well, I hadn't decided. Emerilla maybe, or Antamarie."

I was glad I hadn't ended up with one of my mother's names, a made-up name I had to repeat to everyone all the time. A name that no one could pronounce on the first day of school.

"Or Ruth," she said. "For a while, I thought about naming you Ruth. You know, like the girl in the Bible story, the one who stays with her mother."

Mr. Aimes had taught us the story in Religious Studies class. "It was her mother-in-law," I said. "Her husband died, and she stayed with his mother."

"Whoever," she said. "I always liked that story." She leaned back, looked up at the ceiling. "The best stories are always about loyalty, don't you think?"

"I don't know," I said.

"Or betrayal." She raised her eyebrows. "Betrayal's a good plot, too."

I looked at my face in the side mirror and tried to imagine it with the name Ruth, but I couldn't. It just didn't seem to fit. I thought about the girl, Ruth, in the story and about the other girl, Orpah. Because there was another girl, a sister-in-law. Ruth stayed with Naomi, but Orpah walked away. Ruth was the hero, the story seems clear about that, but I could see Orpah's point, too. She'd had her reasons. I didn't doubt that for a minute.

The morning ended and a hot, salty afternoon set in. The dashboard was so hot, it burned my fingers, and the rear view mirror showed we were sunburned, I on the right side of my face and my mother on the left. Together, we had a complete sunburned face, but apart we looked like clowns.

When three o'clock arrived, we still hadn't seen the truck.

"I'm going to check it," I said. "Maybe it came early." I put my hand on the car door to let myself out.

"Wait," she said.

"I'm not waiting anymore," I snapped. I didn't completely understand the grocery swap, but I understood it enough to see she was doing it in a stupid way.

I got out of the car, and she followed. She pulled some things out of the trunk—gardening gloves and what looked like a large pair of pruning sheers—then she set her shoes down on the road and stepped into them. A breeze rose up off the ocean and blew my shirt. We started walking, but halfway up the hill, she bent down to pick something up.

"Would you look at this? It's an earring," she said. She held it up so that the emerald stone caught the light. "This is quite a find, Lindsey, quite a find. I had a gold-plated pen from Joan I was going to use, but this is much better."

I looked at the earring skeptically. "I guess you could double pierce one of your ears. But it's kind of big, it might not look right next to another one."

"I don't want to wear it," she said. "One earring? That's silly. Why would I wear it?" She held it up a bit higher and we both looked at it again. It winked in the sun like a bright green eye.

I shrugged my shoulders and kept walking. The driveway swirled in front of me in a way that made me feel hot and dizzy. I was probably suffering heat exhaustion.

"You're the silly person," I said.

I hadn't noticed it before, but there was a long, short hedge in front of the house. We could hide inside it, if we had to. If it came to that. My mother put on the pair of yellow gardening gloves she was carrying, and we continued walking up, pretending to be gardeners. The first thing we saw when we walked up to the house was a Styrofoam cooler.

"It's the cooler," my mother said in a triumphant voice. "She puts it out in the morning and they fill it up. We should order our groceries to be delivered. We really should."

"But you're always at home," I said.

"Not always," she said.

"When do you go out?"

"When I go to the supermarket."

I opened up the lid of the cooler and looked inside. The groceries were there.

"I told you," I said.

She shrugged. "Would you look at that."

"What do we do now?"

"We take it."

"What for?" I considered it briefly. I was hungry, but we could get caught. If someone apprehended us with Joan's groceries, it could throw a real glitch in our plan.

"For the grocery swap. That's how it works."

"Or we could eat it," I said.

"The plan isn't to eat it," she said.

This was disappointing, but I wasn't in the mood to ask questions. If she wanted the cooler, she'd take it, with or without my help, so I picked up one end of it and she took the other, and we walked back to the car. After we unloaded the groceries, we put the cooler back in its spot on the ground and stared at it. It looked strangely sad, now that I knew it was empty. I hoped that Joan had something else for dinner.

My mother started to walk back toward the front of the house, so I headed to the back. I crossed the driveway and followed a stone footpath around the house until I came to a fence.

The fence was high, and it had no gate, but I could, by standing on my toes, just manage to look over it. I couldn't see much, just the pool, dry and uncovered (a hole, really) and a large fountain, filled with dirty water, where three long-haired alabaster fairies lounged in various positions, washing their hair. The rest of the yard was bare: dry dirt with spots of wild sea grass and a few bright purple flowers.

I almost missed the rabbit house. The fountain blocked it partially, and I had to pull myself up higher on the fence to get a good look at it. It stood three stories tall, boxy and green, a perfect miniature of the big house except for the fact that it had a wider, bigger door, perfectly suited to accommodate a rabbit's wide bottom. The words *The Rabbit Houdini* looped across the roof in bold, black script. A gray squirrel stood on top of the R, stretching for the rabbit's food dish, batting his paw at a carrot.

"You're a no-good thief," I told him. He looked up at me for a minute, considering it. I left him to his bad business and went back to mine.

My mother was still out front when I got back.

"Careful," she whispered. "She's got a burglar alarm." She pointed to a sign in the grass that said ADT SECURITY.

I pushed my way through a line of bushes until I stood beside her. She motioned at Joan's window, and I squatted down beside it. I peered through the glass and waited for my eyes to adjust to the dark. A velvet couch stood on one side of the room, and a large painting of the ocean hung on the wall. The ottoman crouched at an angle, as if reeling back from some long-ago kick from the couch, and on the mantle, a group of blue and white Lladro dancers stood with toes pointed and arms extended, facing each other in an eternal, unmoving dance. Even from here, through the window, I could smell the dust.

"That must be him." My mother pointed to a movie poster above the fireplace—Saul as Houdini, the magician, dressed all in black. He had a wand in his right hand and a top hat with a rabbit poking out of it in his left. His hair was brown, fastened in the back, and he had a short, square chin. I've always thought the photos of the dead should look different than those of the living. Sadder, or more blank, something. Sometimes they do look different to me.

"Creepy," I said.

"It's not creepy," my mother said. "He's just a man like any other, except he happens to be dead."

"Which you have to admit," I said, "is a distinction."

We walked back to the car.

"Oh well," my mother said as she started the engine. "At least we got the earring and the food."

I pulled a banana out of the cooler and started to peel it open.

My mother lunged to take it away from me and the car swerved, almost sending us down the cliff. "We can't eat the food."

I paused, mid-bite, and waited for her to go on. If what she said made sense, I could still put the banana back.

"Think about it," she said. "We've got the earring and the groceries. It should be obvious."

"It's not obvious," I said.

She shrugged. "Well, I can't explain it then."

She took out her cell phone.

"Hello, this message is for Joan Fields. My name is Kate and I'm one of the customer service managers over at Home Grocer. I'm just calling to let you know that we've run into a small problem with your delivery today. One of our drivers called in sick and will be unable to deliver your groceries as planned this morning, so we've gone ahead and put you into the next available time slot, which is this evening. If this will pose a problem for you, please let us know. Again, I apologize. I hope this will not affect your choice to use Home Grocer in the future."

After she ended the call, I stared at her for several seconds, trying to figure out exactly what it was she'd just done.

"What just happened?" I asked.

"Shh. I have to call Willow now, or Rose. It should be Willow, I think. She's sneakier. She's stronger, too. She'll make a better grocer."

"Willow is going to deliver Joan's groceries?"

She nodded. "She'll have to park at the bottom of the driveway and walk up. Otherwise Joan will see that she doesn't have a truck. It'll be a long walk and she'll have a lot to carry, but we can't help that. Once Willow is inside the house and unloading the groceries, she can hide the earring somewhere, under the corner of a rug or someplace. Then later, when I meet Joan, I can tell her I know that she's lost something. Not only that, I can tell her where to find it."

I thought about it for a minute. It seemed like a good plan to me, better than I'd expected, anyway, but I could see some places where it could go wrong. "What if she doesn't want the grocer to come inside her house?" I asked. "What if she calls the store back and tells them she wants them to deliver the groceries to a cooler tomorrow?"

"If that happens, it's between her and the company. We'll eat the food for dinner tonight, and they'll have to figure it out tomorrow. They'll have to deliver another set of groceries, I guess, if they want to keep her business. But I don't think that will happen. Who wants their groceries to sit around all night? Plus, she might be hungry. Maybe there's something in these bags that she plans to fix for dinner."

I sifted through the contents: tofu and string cheese, more bananas, some bran muffins, lettuce, and a case of vitamin water.

"I don't think so," I said.

"Wait a second, are those potato chips? Would you look at that, a bag of potato chips! Here with all of this health food. I don't think Joan will notice if we take this one little thing."

My mother opened the bag, and I looked out the window. I watched cliffs and seals and the sea swirl by while the road twisted and turned beneath me like the tracks of a roller coaster.

That night, we met with the South Node Ladies in our living room.

"I would have picked a different way to get in the house," Maud said, "but I think it can work. Willow will do the delivery because she looks the most like a man."

"I look like a man?" Willow asked.

"I said, the most like a man," Maud said.

Willow rubbed at the faint mustache above her lip, thinking this over. "It might be true," she said. "But I still don't want to do it."

I walked over to the living room window to shut it, but I could only get it to close part way. I put my hand on the cold pane and looked out. Early evening: black palm trees, dirty sky, the smell of burnt tar. The highway throbbed against the glass like a wild heart. I heard a honk, followed by the loud, long screech of a skid. I couldn't see the car, but I felt my fists tighten. My whole body braced for the crash to come.

"One, two, three, bang," my mother said. She always counted it out. I think she did it to calm herself. When she finished, she generally went outside to help, but this time, the skid trailed off into nothing. The driver must have righted the car and moved on.

For a few seconds, no one spoke. It seemed like a solemn occasion. Finally, Rose said, "I think it should be an actual man who does the delivery."

"Women can do anything men can do," Maud said. "Anything a woman does nowadays is believable."

"It's no treat to drive a delivery truck," my mother said. "It's not a career I would choose, but I'm with Maud. There isn't any reason a woman shouldn't be able to do it if she wants to." She walked over to the window and forced it shut. To me, she said, "You have to lift it a little. Lift then slide. It's easy once you get the hang of it."

"Now hear me out." Rose stood. The shirt she wore had a flowered collar and the print of a teddy bear on it. It looked like something someone much younger—or older—would choose, but somehow, in spite of this, she managed to look very serious in it. She held up her hand to quiet the room. "I'm thinking about that nice boy that Lindsey's dating. That nice, strong, young man. It wouldn't be anything for a boy like that to carry a couple bags up a hill. And doesn't he work in a grocery store? He can wear his uniform."

I turned from the window with a jolt. I couldn't believe I'd just heard what I had. The last thing I wanted to do was to involve Paco. As far as I knew, Paco believed I truly was psychic. I didn't know what he'd think about me if I told him the truth. "Paco has to work tonight," I said. It was true. Paco's father had lost his job a week ago, and Paco had taken additional shifts at the store to help his family.

The women nodded in unison, but they didn't look convinced, so I put it into terms they could understand. "He'd want a cut, if he did it. He'd ask for a share of the money."

"A share!" Rose said. "Just for doing that one little thing. I suppose he would. I didn't think of that." She picked at a piece of lint on her sweater. "We don't need him, then, just his uniform."

I tried to protest, but Maud cut me off. "Willow will do the delivery. No more discussion about it."

No one said anything for a long time. It seemed like a verdict had been given, but then Willow stood straight up.

"I will not deliver the groceries!" she said. "On this point, I absolutely refuse to budge!"

Willow could not be persuaded, whatever anyone said, so in the end, Maud had to ask her nephew to do it. He'd done some church work for her in the past, she said, a task that had included spying and pickpocketing credit cards, and it had gone well and she trusted him. He worked cheaply and quickly and he did a good, thorough job.

In the end, the plan went off without a hitch. Maud's nephew delivered the groceries and hid the earring in a potted cactus on the kitchen windowsill, and my mother called Joan to tell her where to find it. She'd acted suspicious, my mother said, but she seemed to believe it, since, as far as she knew, my mother had never been to her house.

# SIXTEEN

When Paco came over to meet me before school on Monday, he said, "I think your mom stole one of my grocery uniforms."

"Did you get it back?"

He gave me an odd look. "Yes. It's back on the balcony rail where it was drying yesterday, minding its own business, when she walked by it with her laundry basket."

"So everything's okay then," I said.

"I guess so, but it's still kind of strange. And so is your reaction. Most people would say, 'No, my mother didn't steal it.' But you just asked if I got it back."

"Well, I believed you," I snapped. "You said she stole it, so I believed you."

"Calm down," he said. "Let's not forget who the victim is here. I'm the one who suffered grocery uniform theft."

He looked up at the ceiling, at the assortment of plaster angels hanging from the fan, then he bent down to pick up one of my mother's books, *Interviewing the Dead*. "Speaking of the psychic business, I want to ask you something. A favor."

*He's going to ask me to contact his brother again,* I thought. I went over my options. I could tell him the

133

truth, that I couldn't, but he'd probably just think I wouldn't. If he did believe it, he'd know I was a fraud. I was still pondering it when he said, "Would you be willing to do a fortune-teller booth at the school playground fundraiser?"

"You want me to do a fortune booth?" It seemed like I might have gotten off easy. I didn't have to contact his brother, after all. Still, I wasn't sure about this. "I don't know," I said.

"You know people don't mean anything when they call you Fortune, right?"

"I know," I said. "It's not that."

He waited for me to explain, but I couldn't think of a reason other than that I didn't like to tell fortunes to people. It seemed selfish to bring that up when it was for such a good cause, so I said, "Okay, I'll do it."

He left, then, to run back to his apartment and "get something." When he returned, he was carrying a costume: a puffy white shirt and a long purple, glitter-trimmed skirt.

"My cousin wore it last year for Halloween," he said.

I held it up and looked at it skeptically. It wasn't going to be my best look, that I was certain, but if I added some of my mother's dangly gold jewelry, I might be able to pull it off. I changed in the bathroom and walked out, cautiously.

"You look great," he said. "Wait, stay there. I'll take your picture."

A flash went off, and I caught a glimpse of myself in the hall mirror: A thin, dark-haired, gypsy girl in someone's crazy idea of a carnival fortune outfit. I could have been a caricature—no one. I could have been anyone at all. I had the sudden, terrifying thought that I was looking not at myself in a costume, but at my own true, fraudulent heart.

I changed out of the costume, but just before we left for school, I put it in my backpack. I'd have to store it in the theater room. I knew what my mother would say if she saw it. She advocated a normal, natural look for psychic readers, though she didn't always achieve it.

We walked down the steps and along the stone path to Paco's car. Ever since Paco's father had lost his job, he'd been more lenient with his car. We had it pretty much every day now. We weren't more of a couple now that we had a car, but it sometimes felt like that was the case. I put my feet up on the dashboard, and we pulled out of the driveway and bumped up onto Sepulveda. The sun came in through the windows at every angle, the way it does in old, low to the ground cars, and the interior smelled like hot dust and worn leather. The wind made a wild, scattered sound in the taped-up sunroof, but I felt safe and happy in that car in a way I can't describe. I watched the street go by through a small hole in the floor and thought about the many strange things that had happened to put me here, in this exact spot. Would I do it all again? Of course not. But, then again, I might.

"Hey, you kids!" a man in a red bandana called out to us. We were pulling up to the school, but when we saw him, we stopped.

"My car broke down," he said. "Do you have two dollars for gas?"

It was an obvious scam, and one I've never liked. Still, he hadn't asked for much. He looked like he truly could use it for something, so I gave it to him.

"There he goes," Paco said. "Off to buy drugs with your money."

"Maybe," I said. I wanted very much to give someone the benefit of the doubt.

We were still standing beside the car when he walked by again, whistling, carrying a container of gasoline.

When we entered the school, Paco took out a stack of flyers for the upcoming carnival planning party. Everyone took one. A few people even went out of their way, turning around or looping out of the crowd to stand in the small line that had formed in front of the door. Paco handed me a stack, and I tried to give them out, too, but I couldn't pull the pages apart fast enough. A stocky boy from the math club offered to help. He walked a pile over to the dance team, who swished over to hand a few to the group of stringy-haired, pack-a-day smokers who huddled at the corner of the blacktop during class. Everybody took one. A few people even said thank you. There's something about building a playground for kids, I guess, that everyone just agrees is a good thing.

The bell rang just as we finished, but we took our time getting our stuff together. The playground seemed worth being late for. After everyone left, I stood for a second in a slant of light from the hallway window. I thought, *There, at the end of the hall is my locker. My homeroom class. My boyfriend disappearing down the hall.* It seemed too ordinary, too good to be true. I clutched my books against my chest, as if I could, by gripping tight enough, hold on to it all a little longer.

That night, out on the balcony, I said to Paco. "If I had to leave . . . If, say, something happened and I had to leave so fast that I couldn't even say goodbye, I want you to know it wouldn't be because I wanted to."

"What could happen?" he asked. He pushed his easel back and swirled some paint around. I was afraid to look at the canvas. His work always looked angry to me.

"Anything. It's hypothetical." I was thinking about the police catching up with us, tracking my mother down, but of course, I couldn't say that. I put my legs through the metal railing and let them hang over the side of the balcony in the windy dark.

"You better say goodbye if you leave," he said.

"Right. But I'm talking about if I couldn't. In the hypothetical situation that I'm talking about, I'd have to leave very quickly and I wouldn't be able to talk to anyone."

"I don't want to talk about hypotheticals anymore," he said. "You can look now. It's ready."

I knew before I even looked at the picture that I would hate it. I disliked all of his work, but the strength of my reaction took me by surprise. The painting was simple enough: me, alone, in front of the Sepulveda Apartments in the fortune costume he'd brought me. I looked very uneasy in it. I had a blank, misplaced look on my face. Also, I had no eyes.

"Why don't I have any eyes?" I asked. The picture bothered me more than I could explain. "Have I been hurt? Did someone poke out my eyes?" I crossed my arms and glared at Paco. This picture was just not flattering. How could I look nice without any eyes?

"I never give people all of their pieces," Paco said. "I have a whole series of my mother without a stomach. Get it? All those pregnancies and no stomach."

"No," I said. "I don't."

"It's just something I do," he said.

He took out an airbrush and sprayed another sky over the first, a liquid, washed-out Los Angeles blue, and I looked back at the canvas, not convinced.

"I'm going inside," I said.

Later, he knocked on the door, and presented the picture to me again, but he had to turn my head to make me look at it. I had eyes now, but they were green and he'd covered my lids with purple eye shadow.

"Better," I said. "But I never wear that shade." I stared at him for a minute in the semidarkness, crossing my arms. I was still unhappy.

"I wish you wouldn't take it personally," he said. "You know, I almost didn't give you arms, but then I remembered how you said you thought you needed glasses the other day. Remember? We were sitting on the steps and you said, 'I can't see one word of that sign. I must need glasses.'"

I didn't remember.

We started at each other in the dark for a minute, then he said, "If you left, I'd really miss you. That's the answer to your question."

"I'd miss you, too," I said.

I wondered if love was this worrisome of a thing for everyone, and if it was, then why was everyone so fanatical about it? Paco leaned forward. His lips were warm, but slightly chapped, and he tasted like the grape soda we had been drinking earlier. I must have stepped back, because he had to lean forward to kiss me again, and when he did, his head bumped into an angel. That angel bumped into another, and both started spinning, and the eyes of our crescent moon clock popped open. "It's twelve o'clock," it chimed. "It's twelve o'clock." It looked around the room with its weird roving eyes and sang its strange, twinkly song.

We might have made up. We might have forgotten we'd fought at all, if Paco hadn't pulled something out of his shirt pocket.

"Here," he said. "I want to show you the website I made."

I looked down at the printout he was holding. The words SPRING CARNIVAL ran in bold, wobbly letters across the top. Below this, slightly off-center, and surrounded by multicolor links, was the photo he'd taken of me the other day in my gypsy carnival suit.

"Please tell me this isn't on the Internet."

"It's a good picture of you. Look, you have eyes."

"I see that. But is it on the Internet?" I was starting to really panic now. People were looking for my mother. I couldn't just show up online. "Because I can't be on the Internet. I absolutely can't."

"Hey," he said. "Calm down, okay?"

This was the *wrong* thing to say to me. I felt like this comment took the focus off the situation, off the terrible thing he had done, and aimed it, instead, at my mood. I didn't want to derail the conversation in this way, so I said, very clearly, very slowly, "Is this or is this not online?"

"I didn't put it up yet. No," he said. He made a big show of balling the paper up and throwing it into the trash. I watched the lid swing back and forth several times, before I felt myself breathe again.

He moved toward me in the dark and put his hand on my shoulder. He tried to look at my face, but I wouldn't turn my head. "Something's up with you," he said. "Something about your situation isn't right."

"You don't just put someone's picture on the Internet. You don't."

"Well, I see that," he said.

We were quiet again, and then he said, "I get this feeling sometimes like you're lying to me."

"You're saying I'm a liar now?" I was sensitive about that, I guess. I guess I'd worried about it some myself. "That's great. That's super."

I turned around and crossed my arms. I waved at him to go away, but he came up behind me and put his chin on my shoulder. I felt his breath on my neck, the thump of his heart on my back.

"What are you running from, Lindsey?" he whispered.

I thought about telling him the truth. I could almost feel the relief I'd experience from doing so. But then I remembered, again, the promise I'd made to my mother. I held my shoulders and arms very stiff until he let go.

"I'm not running away from anything," I said.

I was pretty sure we both knew I was lying. I worried he might be angry beyond repair, that I might lose him, but then he said, "I didn't actually do anything wrong. We're clear on that, right?"

I nodded.

"Because it's not like I actually put it up."

"You didn't," I said.

"Okay," he said. "As long as we have that straight. "

He kissed me on the forehead and walked out the door. I listened to him whistling as he made his way across the balcony, the sound growing higher and softer, then the thump of his door as he shut it. The quick way he'd forgotten about the argument made me wish I had more men in my life. A father would be nice, maybe a brother. The South Node Ladies could complain about men all they wanted, but I knew the truth. Women were the more difficult, complicated ones.

# SEVENTEEN

The carnival planning party was at eight o'clock the next night at Paco's place. I was on my way out the door when my mother stopped me. She looked up from what I'd begun to think of as her permanent spot on the couch and said, "Where are you going?"

"To Paco's."

She sighed. "But they're calling for rain again."

It seemed like she could use some cheering up, so I said, "They're always wrong."

"You think so?" she said.

"Yes," I said, although I could hear the first drops.

She pulled a ratty red afghan up to her chin and burrowed further into the slump of the couch. "I thought we'd watch the pageant videos. Watch the ceiling get wet and sink."

"That sounds great and all," I said, "but I can't."

I put my hand back on the doorknob and prepared, again, to escape, but she said, "Wait."

I stopped, but she didn't say anything else.

"Why don't you call the South Node Ladies?" I said. "Invite them over."

"Maybe," she said.

The phone rang and she picked it up. "Tarot Hotline. Yes, hold please."

It was one of her tricks to make people wait on the phone. That way she racked up the seconds and made more money. Sometimes, she told them to get things—pencils or markers or sweet-smelling fruits—to waste more time.

"You should deal with that," I said.

She nodded. "What time will you be home?"

"Couple hours," I said.

She picked up the phone. "Thank you for holding. Have I read for you before?"

I closed the door and started across the balcony to Paco's apartment. The rain came down around me in a hard, sudden way, turning the balcony into a tunnel. It made me think of the mazes my mother and I used to build, years ago, for my stuffed animals. We used blocks and sticks and toilet paper rolls, anything we could find, and we'd put treats and balls in the center. Sometimes, I'd get so wrapped up in the mazes that if a friend knocked on the door, I'd send them away so I could keep playing with my mother. The sad part was, when I started the sixth grade, those mazes started to look crazy to me. At night, on my wall, their shadows loomed like a twisted dream, a type of living nightmare for stuffed animals. When I found out that some girls from my school were coming over, I had thrown them away, just smashed them all up in the trash.

I turned the corner of the long balcony and stopped. Sydney and Paco were standing, together, outside the door beneath the porch light.

"Put the drinks out here," Sydney said. "That way they stay cold. Where are the chips?" She bent over, arranging the cooler.

"Somewhere," Paco said. "I don't know. Maybe I don't have chips."

They were only planning the party. I could see that, but every word they said, every motion they made, seemed oddly unreal, as if I were watching them on a movie screen or from across some great sweeping distance. I thought, if I have to leave L.A., this is how it will all work out. Paco will be with Sydney. I felt very sure of it.

Paco looked up and waved.

"Hey," I said. I walked over and stood beside him.

He leaned in toward me. "Hey, you."

Sydney sneered. She slunk off inside, but the musky scent of her perfume remained, hovering in the rain between us.

"I like your hair like this," Paco said. He picked up a piece of my hair and pushed it behind my ear.

"You mean rained on?" I said.

Lightning flashed above the pool and Paco turned toward it.

"Did you see that?" he asked.

I laughed. People in L.A. were always overly impressed with lightning.

"What's funny?" he said.

Sydney poked her head out the door and asked, "Was that lightning?"

Paco and Sydney talked for a while about how bright and fantastic they thought lightning was, then Sydney said, "It wasn't as bad as the one that shook the store the other day. Was it Paco?"

"Lightning doesn't shake places," I told her. "Thunder does."

When she went inside, I said to Paco, "So, Sydney visits you at the store?"

I didn't want to act jealous, but I couldn't help it. It bothered me.

"Nah," he said. "Just if she's there already, you know, shopping." He moved some sodas around in the cooler.

I might have pushed it some more, but we'd had that fight yesterday, so I told myself it wasn't anything.

"Let's just go to the party," I said. The wind blew a fistful of rain at us when we started for the door.

Inside, the air was thick and hot. A few people sat on Paco's couch, in front of the TV, but most were on the floor, working on posters in small groups. I found Emily with her back against the china cabinet, next to a cardboard cutout of a polka-dotted clown. When she saw me, she turned and the row of teacups behind her shook.

"Look at this thing I got stuck with," she said. "Can you draw?"

"No," I told her. "I'm terrible."

"Me too," she said.

I started toward her. At first, Paco followed me, but Scott threw a balled-up paper at him. He walked over to mock wrestle the paper, which turned out to be his report card, from Scott, and I sat down next to Emily.

"Guess what," Emily said. "I kissed Scott tonight."

"Really?"

She nodded. "He was sitting there, over there," she pointed, "watching his game show, acting like a conceited idiot like he always does, and I thought, why not? I think he's still reacting from the shock of it." She lifted her paintbrush and drew a striped hat on the clown.

"I didn't know you liked him," I said.

"I didn't either," she said. "I always thought he annoyed me. All that stupid game show trivia. I always kind of thought he looked at everyone like they don't have a brain."

"He does look at everyone like that," I said.

I looked over at Scott. He was, right now, sitting in front of the TV, leaning forward, shouting his answers at the screen. Behind him, on the other side of the couch, the window rattled. A shape appeared—the long shadow of a woman.

"Is that your mom?" Emily said.

"No," I lied. *She's lonely*, I thought. I wished she would just go away.

"Hey," someone yelled, "someone's mom just peeked in."

"Yeah," someone else said, "a mom in a crazy rain hat."

"You need to get control of your mother," Emily said. "Put down some boundaries or something."

"I don't think she's that kind of mom," I said. "There's really no hope for her."

She paused, still holding her paintbrush. "My mom used to have this stupid idea that I could be a child actress. I did a commercial once, for lemonade, and a print ad for Gap Kids. Maybe you saw it?"

I shook my head.

"Well I'm bigger now. You might not have realized it was me. She tried to get me into the movies for a while. She'd take me to all of these auditions, pull me out of school, set me up on the stage. I'd sing, dance, read lines. When I finished, some stuffy, stupid guy in dorky clothes would always say no, sorry. Too old, too young, too cutesy, not cute enough. I used to come home afterward and just take out all of this food and just eat: cookies, doughnuts, entire cakes, anything I could get my hands on. The audition people started to say, too fat, then, but she'd make me go anyway. She'd just scoop me up, kicking and yelling, and put me in the car. One day, I guess I must have been around five, she bent down to lift me like she always did, but she couldn't. I'd gotten too heavy. My will was stronger than hers. Everything changed between us after that."

I looked up. My mother was inside now, standing in the doorway in rain boots and a huge windbreaker jacket. "Lindsey," she said. "Get up. We're going. I can't stand one more second in that hell hole."

I stood and walked toward the door, accompanied by jeers and a collective *ooooh*.

I smiled brightly, as if nothing at all embarrassing or even remotely out of the ordinary had happened, but as soon as I shut the door behind me, I shouted. "You have no right to come in there like that. No right!"

"What?" She looked genuinely surprised.

"You can't just show up like that when I'm with my friends. The fact that you don't know why is the reason why."

She twisted her mouth, considering this. She started to walk away, taking giant, clunking steps down the metal stairs, and I followed her, still shouting.

"It started coming in, again," she said over my voice, "the rain. Into the bedroom this time. I didn't know if I was inside or outside anymore so I thought, I'll just go get Lindsey and we'll head out to the Beverly Hills Hotel for a nice change."

I softened a little. I didn't like the leaks either. I looked away from her and out at the courtyard. The rain had stopped, but it still clung to the leaves of the palm trees.

It made a rushing, leaving sound in the gutter spouts of the apartment.

"Did Joan invite us?" I asked hopefully. My mother had mentioned earlier that Joan was staying there now. Her house had been in a mudslide, and it was being rebuilt.

"Not in so many words."

It didn't sound promising, but I followed her to the car anyway. I couldn't go back to the party after the way I had left, and I did not want to go back to the apartment. I glanced over my shoulder at it. The last light bulb we had, one we'd stolen from an abandoned apartment downstairs, was flickering inside. The windows flashed on and off like yellow teeth.

We drove down Sepulveda in silence. At one point, we came to a complete stop to let a group of teenage girls cross in front of us. The girls wore short skirts, T-shirts, and white-wedged sandals—the right clothes—and I thought, looking at them, that their lives, like their clothes, were normal in a way that mine was not. They were safe, somehow, in a way that I was not. At the exact same time, I realized with some alarm that I could still smell our apartment. It was there in the car with us, in my clothes and my hair. It couldn't have been any worse if I'd come up from the mud and the dead or out of some grungy pond, the way ghosts did in the late-night horror movies my mother and I liked to watch on TV.

The Beverly Hills Hotel looked just as it did in the movies. Tall and proud and well preserved, still its signature pink after all these years. We followed a red carpet up the steps and through the open doors. In the lobby, curved couches faced a giant chandelier and palm plants stretched long fingers up beside white columns. A vase of pink flowers stood, perfectly arranged, at the center of the room. I wanted to touch one, but I thought my fingers might ruin it. My flip-flops looked cheap and sad on the polished floor.

"Don't let your jaw drop like that," my mother said. "They'll think we don't belong here."

I nodded, but when she turned away, I looked around the room again. I'd never set foot in it, but the very strange feeling that I'd seen it before settled over me. Most likely I had. If you think you've seen something before in Los Angeles, you probably have: you've seen it in the movies or on TV. My mother must have felt it, too, because she leaned over and whispered, "It feels like coming home."

Joan wasn't staying in the main building of the hotel, but in something called a bungalow, which meant she had her very own secluded pink house. We had to walk through the garden to get to it, along a carpeted path. When we knocked, she opened the door in her bathrobe, holding a white spotted rabbit the size of a cat.

"What a surprise," she said. "Did you call? I haven't checked my phone."

We shook our heads.

"What a surprise," she said again. She shifted the rabbit in her arms and held out one of his paws to me. "Shake hands with her, Houdini."

I shook the rabbit's hand, and she set him down. He hopped off, and we followed Joan into the living room. In this room, gold predominated—gold walls stood behind a gold couch and two gold-striped chairs—but it was a careful, muted gold and it wasn't glitzy. The furniture surrounded a glass table in a careful, conversational way, and a log burned low in the fireplace. We sat down on the couch, and Joan sat down across from us, cross-legged, in one of the striped chairs.

For a moment, we just looked at each other, and then Joan said, "I'm completely alone."

When she said it, the room drew in. The very air around her seemed to take a breath. *I will carry this image with me, always,* I thought, and on bad days, it will rise up. It will bubble up to the surface and turn to face me with all of the inherent power of bad choices and old guilt. Joan on the chair with her hands on her face. I closed my eyes, but it would not go away.

We stayed in the bungalow with Joan for several hours, talking and eating macaroons off a silver platter, until finally Joan yawned and said, "It's late. I hate to be the one to end the party, but I should get some sleep."

A few seconds passed while she waited for us to get up and leave.

"I suppose we should go home, Lindsey," my mother said. "Deal with those leaks."

Joan yawned again. "What leaks?"

"Oh, I don't want to bother you with it."

"Are you talking about leaks in your ceiling, Debbie? As in water coming through?"

"It's not that bad," my mother said.

"Oh good. You had me worried there for a second." Joan stood up from her chair and stretched. I stood, too, but my mother remained in place.

"Actually, it is bad." My mother bit her lip in a worried way. "I don't know why I'm trying to cover it up."

"Is it bad or not?" Joan asked.

"There are leaks all over," I said. "It's disgusting."

"Lindsey!" my mother said.

"Sorry," I said.

"Goodness!" Joan said. "Well, you two are welcome to stay here."

"Are you sure?" my mother said in her most unassuming voice. "We wouldn't want to put you out."

"Of course I'm sure. It's just me in this big place." She waved her arm in a giant semicircle. "Who else would care?"

"Well, it would be a big relief to us," my mother said.

Joan smiled. "Please. I insist. Stay as long as you need to. Make yourselves at home."

We took her advice. My mother put her coat in the closet and carried her purse to the spare bedroom, and I settled in on the couch. After everyone had fallen asleep, I went to the window and peeked out. The sky had cleared enough to see a few stars. A yellow moon, tipped on its back like a casualty, ducked in and out of a swirl of clouds. I took my notebook out of my purse and wrote:

*Horned Moon. The type that is said to cradle water and predict drought. A very good sign we've seen the last of this rain.*

# EIGHTEEN

Our first morning at the Beverly Hills Hotel, Joan's alarm clock rang at 5:00, 5:15, 5:30, 5:45, and 6:00. I drifted in and out of sleep, catching and re-catching my dreams, until eventually I gave up. I looked up at the strange, bright ceiling and listened to the sounds Joan made—the water running in the toilet, the shower, the sink, the slam of the cabinet door—with the kind of prickly feeling that I thought might be a genuine premonition.

*We shouldn't be here*, I thought. *It doesn't feel right.*

I must have fallen asleep again after that, because when I woke up, Joan was sitting at the bottom of my couch with a bowl of cereal. She had a different hotel robe on now, a larger one that she seemed to sink into, and a towel that wound around her head like a fat pink turban. Her legs were bare, egg white where they poked out from beneath her robe, but the skin around her eyes was dark and yellow. When she noticed I was awake, she nearly dropped her bowl on her lap. For a second, we just looked at each other. I don't know which of us was more shocked, but then she turned back to her breakfast, and I rolled over.

For what seemed like a very long time, I lay very still beside her, listening to her eat: *clink, slurp, clink, slurp,* and her spoon scraped the bottom of the bowl. It rang in my head like an off-key bell. All noise is solitary at predawn, when the world is dark and even the birds are asleep, but hers seemed particularly so.

*What are we doing here?* I thought. *What kind of people are we?*

I put a pillow over my head and waited for her to go away.

When I woke again, it was noon. Joan was gone, and I no longer had the sinking premonition I'd felt when the alarm went off. I heard a scratching sound and turned. The rabbit was hopping toward me in wide, white pants and a sweater that said, THE BEVERLY HILLS HOTEL.

"Did I scare you?" I asked him.

I half expected him to answer; he looked so smart in his sweater. But my mother spoke instead.

"He drinks bottled water and eats organic vegetables. I saw what she left out for his lunch."

"Where is she?" I asked.

"She went to see someone about her house. Do you know there's a television set in the bathroom?" she said. "The bathroom! And just look at this comforter!" She thrust one of the bed blankets at me, but when I moved to touch it, she pulled it away. "It's Matelassé fabric. Matelassé fabric! And there's pink Grecian marble and Italian granite in the bathroom!"

"Right," I said. I didn't know much about fabrics or granite, and I didn't think she did either. Sometimes she knew the names of things, but most of the time she lied.

I hopped off the couch and walked toward her. "Ah, but if you look closely at this comforter, you can tell that it's actually a very unusual silk from the Orient. The slight discoloration of this corner, here, shows me that real silk worms spun this."

"You think so? Silk, huh?" She bent forward, squinting at it, even though I'd made it all up. "You're right. I can tell by the watermarks how long it took the worms to make it. This took ten years."

I didn't call her out on the lie. She just seemed too happy. She flung open the curtain, and the bright blue sky washed in. "This is how the rich live," she said. "Get used to it."

I didn't think I could. I had the odd idea that the gold walls would not stay up if I touched them, that the plush carpet wouldn't support the weight of my feet. I couldn't shake the thought that I was looking at stolen light.

We spent the afternoon outside, beside the pool. It was a hot, breezeless day, full of thin air and the kind of bright, California light that heightens color and can bleach out shadows. We found two striped chairs together and sat down. After a minute or two, a waiter approached us and asked for our order.

"Oh, yes," my mother said. "We'll have two Cobb salads." She said it in an official but offhand voice, the way she must have imagined people here spoke when they ordered, but when she finished, she leaned toward me and whispered, "The big thing to do at the Beverly Hills Hotel is order a Cobb salad by the pool."

"I don't want a Cobb salad," I said.

The waiter raised his eyebrows. He must have been waiting for me to say what I did want, but my mother answered instead.

"She'll have the Cobb salad, too. Trust me on this one, Lindsey."

"I'll have a hamburger," I said.

The waiter looked back and forth at us with a forced smile on his face, then he disappeared. He fled, actually, and my mother said, "Keep your eyes peeled for movie stars. You know, we really should set up a psychic table out here."

It sounded like a terrible idea to me. It sounded like an idea that could get us kicked out of the hotel, so I said, "We're not setting up a psychic table."

"Well not this second."

We were quiet for a few minutes. I texted with Paco, and she read a magazine, but after a while she said, "Do you remember what Joan's father's name was? It was James, right?"

"It was Tom." We'd looked this up online two days ago. I'd answered this exact question seven times, but she still thought Tom's name was James.

"That's what I thought," she said. "I'm going to really wow her with that fact tonight when she gets home."

I imagined her calling him James, the disaster of that. It seemed highly unlikely to me that she was going to wow anyone.

"Right," I said. "You do that."

She put her sunglasses back on and leaned back in her chair. "Why do you always have to say *right* like that, Lindsey? Like it's anything but right? It's annoying."

"Right," I said.

"Stop being so stupid. This is important. Tonight is information night. Tonight is the night we're impressing Joan with all the information we've been saving up, so get ready!"

"Right," I said again.

I wasn't as excited about information night as she was. Information night irritated me, particularly since she'd just gotten the name of Joan's father wrong. I rolled away from her, onto my stomach, and tried not to think about it anymore. My face felt hot, and my eyes hurt from the sun. The backs of my eyelids stung. I'd sweat so much that my towel had stuck to the back of my shirt when I'd turned over, and I wondered if this broke some kind of rule. I didn't think people were allowed to sweat at the Beverly Hills Hotel. The people in front of me, in the pool and on the other striped chairs, looked cool and glamorous. Models, maybe, or movie stars on vacation. If the women spilled out of bathing suits, it was out of the top only, and all of the men had muscles. Even the children were better looking than average. I watched a young blond woman pull two round-faced toddlers out of the pool and tried to recollect the movie or magazine cover where I'd last seen her face.

The rich are no better than the poor. In many ways they're worse, everyone knows that, but they *are* better looking. Especially at the Beverly Hills Hotel. I felt as if I'd wandered onto a soap opera set or a scene from a movie, a place where a casting director had handpicked all the people. Certainly, the percentage of beautiful people to the merely average was off by a great deal. When I looked down at my stomach, it seemed to grow in front of me. My thighs blew up like two balloons.

My mother gazed at me in a measuring way from over the top of her sunglasses. "You're burning, Lindsey," she said, exasperated.

"You too," I said. "You look like a lobster."

"No. I'm just a little flushed with heat."

"I'm flushed, too," I said. But I ordered some suntan lotion anyway and charged it to the room.

I watched her eye me suspiciously as I slathered it on. She wants me to be strong, I thought. She wants me to have what it takes to stand up to whatever assaults me, be it the sun or whatever. She likes to imagine that she has taught me how to survive in the world on my own, without much protection from her or anyone else. She likes to imagine I don't need her, almost as much as she likes to imagine I do. This way, she feels free to leave me at any time. It didn't matter, though, because I knew the truth: there was no way she would ever let me go. I squirted more lotion on my hand and rubbed it on my skin until I looked like a snowman.

"You look ridiculous," she said. She rolled over and shut her eyes, shutting me out.

When we finished at the pool, my mother wanted to go to the Polo lounge, but I was hot and I wanted to go back to the bungalow. We fought about it for a few minutes, but in the end she gave in. We left our towels on our chairs and started back.

After the bright sun, the bungalow felt like an icebox, and it smelled like a florist's refrigerator. When my mother opened the door, goose bumps popped up all over my body, and the hair on my arms stood up on end.

"Something's wrong with the temperature," I said. "Did you turn the air up or something?"

"Isn't it great!" my mother said. "We can keep this room as cool as we want!" At the Sepulveda Apartment Complex, we hadn't had any heat, let alone air-conditioning, so it seemed like a real treat. It had been a dream of ours, always, to be in a situation where cost didn't matter.

"I'm going to turn it down," I said.

"Do what you want. I'm going to go back to the apartment and grab our stuff. Want to come?"

I wanted to take a shower, so I said no, but as soon as she left, I regretted it. It seemed strange to be at the hotel without her.

I stepped into the shower and turned the water on. It came down hot, but I gradually relaxed into it. I looked at the line-up of small bottles in front of me, the shampoos and conditioners and body gels, and picked up each one. I turned them around, studying them, then I squeezed them into my hand and mixed them together with my fingers. They smelled bad like that, all blended—a bit like the aggressive, flowery women that sell perfume at department stores. The ones that spring out from the backs of glass-topped counters and accost you with spray bottles.

"Would you like to try a fragrance?" I asked myself.

"I might as well," I answered myself, "because certainly I can. Certainly, I can afford any of them."

I was in a pretty good mood until I stepped out of the shower and Sydney called.

"Hi," she said, "It's Sydney."

"Hi," I said. I was still dripping wet. "How did you get my number?" I'd asked not to be listed in the school directory for safety reasons, so I really didn't know.

"I called Paco to get it," she said.

"Of course you did," I said.

I told her to hold for a second, but I ended up taking longer than that. I guess I wasn't in any particular hurry. I got dressed slowly and walked outside with the phone, still wringing out my hair. The sun had gone down; the air had an edge of a chill to it. The hotel was lit and pink against the sky. I walked down the path to the pool and sat down on one of the chairs before I let her know I was listening again.

"Oh hi." She sounded surprised to hear my voice. I was surprised to hear hers, too. I had been hoping she would have hung up. I traced my finger along the stripes of the chair and waited for her to speak.

"I just wanted to call and say I'm sorry," she said. "You know, about the cards and the purse and telling everyone you were wearing my old uniform and all that."

It seemed odd, her apologizing all of a sudden like that. I didn't completely believe it.

"Did you hear my apology?"

"I did," I said.

"So we're friends then? Right?"

I considered this. She'd apologized. I'd forgiven her. But I wasn't sure it meant we had to be friends.

"Okay," I said finally.

"It means a lot to me, Lindsey, thanks."

"Okay," I said. "Well, I'll see you at school."

But before I could hang up, she spoke again.

"About that," she said. "I used to sit with Emily and Scott at lunch when I was dating Paco. Did you know that?"

I did, so I said yes.

"Well, when we broke up, it was like I lost my friends, too. Anyway, I'm thinking of maybe eating lunch with you guys again, sometimes. What do you think?"

I'd accepted her apology. It seemed like I had to at least act like I'd forgiven her now, but somehow, I couldn't quite bring myself to do it.

"I don't think it will really work out all that well if you eat lunch with us," I said.

She was quiet for a second, but then she must have decided to ignore my comment, because she changed the subject. "Paco told me about how you're going to read tarot cards at the fair. I think that's really cool."

"Thanks," I said. The wind blew across the patio, rippling the pool water, and I shivered. I put my hand on my hair. It felt stiff now, in addition to being cold and wet. I pulled my sweatshirt down and tucked my legs inside, stretching it to fit. "I have to go."

"Yeah? Well, okay. I'll see you at lunch then," she said and hung up.

I took my tarot cards out of my purse and laid them out in the moonlight. After a while, I turned one over. The fool, I guessed, but the card was the Two of Cups reversed: communication breakdowns, opposing opinions, false friends.

I was still holding the card when I walked back inside. My mother was back, now, and so was Joan. They were sitting on the floor, drinking white wine and talking in silly, slow voices, while the rabbit hopped between them with the cork.

"Some spirits are louder than others," my mother said. "Lindsey will tell you. Well, maybe not. She doesn't hear dead people like I do. What I have is called clairaudience. It means I hear voices. Lindsey has something different. I'm not sure what you call what Lindsey has."

"I have the same thing," I said. I didn't like it when she tried to act special. My mother frowned. She waved to the hall, indicating I should go there, but I sat down beside them instead. Joan slid back to let me in.

"I think Saul is trying to get through to me," my mother said, "but a louder, more dominant spirit keeps stepping in. Have you lost anyone else, Joan? Wait. Don't answer. Have you lost anyone whose name begins with a T?"

Joan looked at her suspiciously. "My father."

"Yes," she said. "The spirit could be a father. Sometimes he speaks in a stern voice. But caring. He sounds caring."

"My father wasn't stern or caring."

"Hmm," my mother thought that over. "Whoever it is has a pain in their chest."

Joan set down her drink. "My father died of a heart attack. She looked at my mother out of the corner of her eye. "I feel like I might have told you that."

The room felt too hot, and I shifted uncomfortably. This was going even worse than I thought it would.

My mother began to talk quickly, the way she always did when caught in a lie. "Hold on. I'm getting something from Saul. He wants to know, are you wearing the necklace?"

This was a real jump. We didn't know for certain the necklace Joan was wearing was from Saul. It turned out it wasn't. But that didn't seem to matter.

161

"The dolphin necklace," Joan said. "No, I'm not, Saul. I'm sorry. I'll go get it. Don't go."

She spoke to the empty ceiling with such a sad, eager expression, that a wave of pain shot through me. I wanted very much to point out to her exactly how ludicruous all of it was, but I didn't know how.

Joan scurried off to her room, and my mother leaned back and took a long, deep breath. She must have thought she'd just made a narrow escape.

I pulled the Two of Cups card out of my pocket and set it down in front of her, reversed. False friends. She'd know what it meant. It wouldn't do either of us any good to deny it was the card we held.

# NINETEEN

A few days after my mother and I moved into the hotel, the police showed up at the Sepulveda Complex. I was visiting Paco at the time. We were sitting on the balcony across from what I now considered my old apartment when I noticed the tops of their hats below us on the path. One officer was tall, the other short and wide. The tall one had a brighter hat. They didn't seem to be in any particular hurry. Their shoes made a loud, careless sound when they started up the metal steps.

I watched them knock on my old door, then I ducked into the laundry room. After a second or two, Paco followed.

"Don't talk," I told him. I sat down on the floor, in front of the dryer, and let it thump against my back.

Paco studied me for a second or two. He put his head to the side and narrowed his eyes, the way he did sometimes when faced with a difficult homework problem, but then he must have given up trying to solve me, because he sat down on the ground and put his arm around my shoulder.

"Are we hiding?" he whispered.

I nodded.

"From the police?"

"Yes," I whispered.

The dryer went off. The constant thumping sound disappeared, and I could hear the erratic beat of my own heart. I tried to remember what Paco had just asked me.

He stood, walked to the door, and looked out.

"Duck down," I whispered. "What are you doing?"

"They're leaving," he said. "They're gone."

He sat back down beside me. "Are you going to explain it to me now?"

I took a deep breath and told him all of it, even the parts I didn't understand. I told him about the fire, how I was pretty sure my mother had set it. And I told him about Barney Wilcox and the money he'd buried, the way she'd admitted to me that she'd dug it up. I described how we'd packed in a hurry, the fast way we'd driven away. I told him about the Documents for a New Life website, and I told him my real name.

"I don't understand," he said finally.

"I don't fully understand it either."

"Which one of those things do you think the police want her for?"

I shrugged. "I don't know for sure. Maybe all of them."

He leaned back against the dryer, considering it. "But why wouldn't she just tell you what she did? Why make you wonder?"

*If I understood that*, I thought, *it would make everything simpler.*

"It's just how she is," I said.

He was quiet for a minute, then he said, "I hope you don't have to leave."

"I hope not," I said.

I worried about telling my mother about the police. Who knew what crazy thing she might do? But at the same time, I still had the irrational belief she could fix things. I thought if I carried the problem to her like a doll, upside down and by its one remaining leg, she might take it from me and detangle its hair and figure out how to make it right.

But when we pulled up to the hotel, Paco said, "You should think about what you want to do before you ask her about it. I don't want you to take this the wrong way, but I think something might be wrong with her. The things she does. Her whole mental process, it's off."

"I know," I said. "I know it's off."

Beside us, cars gathered—a honking, soot spitting, bright metal mess—but our car stayed still. He put his hand on top of mine, and I leaned onto his shoulder. I didn't want to leave him. Not yet.

"I want to stay," I said. "For as long as possible. That's my decision."

I don't think I realized exactly how much I meant it until I saw the way it made him smile.

When I found my mother, she was standing on the hotel garden path, staring up at a banana tree.

"Would you look at that bird," she said. "That's a caged bird. You know what? I think someone must have lost that bird."

A bright, lime green parakeet hopped down from the tree and landed on the carpeted path. He took a few hops forward, and my mother stepped toward him. "I'm going to catch him," she proclaimed. She leaned forward and swooped down, but she missed him by a foot. The parakeet looked back at her before he hopped away.

"I need to talk to you," I said.

She took a step toward the bird.

"I'm talking to you, bird catcher," I said.

"But the bird?"

"Forget the bird. The bird doesn't matter."

She looked down at the bird, then up at me as if she were trying to pick between us. "To someone he does. I bet whoever lost that bird doesn't think that bird doesn't matter."

She walked away and I followed. My sneakers made a squishing sound on the carpeted path.

"The police were at the Sepulveda apartment," I said.

She stopped. For a second, she seemed to think very hard about it, but then she began to walk again.

"Aren't you even worried?" I asked.

"Of course I am. But what can we do? We can't leave now. We're so close to getting Joan's money."

"Right," I said. I was relieved to hear it. But then I thought about what the decision might mean, about what might happen to her if we stayed. "What if they find you?"

"They won't," she said. "We're in a pretty safe place, don't you think? Checked in at the hotel under Joan's name."

, "I guess so." I wanted to believe it.

The bird squawked and flew away. It moved through the air in a clumsy zigzag pattern until it was just a small, bright green dot in the pale wide sky. We watched it until we couldn't see it anymore, then my mother said, "You didn't have to frighten the bird. Now, why did you have to go and frighten the bird?"

She walked faster, swinging her arms in a random, looping way until I started to feel frightened, too. *What did she do?* I wondered. *What was she capable of? Was it possible it was worse than I'd thought?*

She kept walking. She stepped out from the dense jungle of foliage and onto the grass, into the hard, glittering, brilliant sun, and for a second I saw her clearly. Not as my mother, but as someone else, her own self. For a second, I saw her exactly the way she was.

We didn't speak for the rest of the afternoon. She left to pick up her check from the phone line and I worked on some financial aid forms for college. I finally went to bed at 3 a.m, but a couple minutes later, my mother walked into the living room and woke me.

"I can't sleep," she whispered. "Can you sleep?"

"Yes," I said. "Go away."

She nudged me, tickled me under my arms, until I rolled away from her. "Are you mad at me?" she asked.

"I am mad at you," I said.

"You are?" She'd asked the question, but she looked surprised.

"You don't tell me anything and you didn't even ask me what I wanted to do about the police."

"I knew you were mad," she said, like she'd solved some great mystery. She sat down on the couch, and I felt myself slide down into the hole her body made.

"The thing is," I told her, "you make really bad decisions. Like burning down the house. And I make good ones. Or I feel like I could, anyway, but you never ask me."

I waited for her to deny setting the house on fire, but she didn't. She just looked at me out of the corner of her eye in a confused way, like I was just now telling her something new.

"Okay," she said, finally. "What do you want to do? Do you want to just give up the money and go?"

"I want to stay."

She snapped her fingers. "Good decision, Lindsey. It just so happens to be the exact same decision as mine."

I laughed. It was so much better when we agreed.

"It's just lucky we were here when they came," she said.

Poor Joan, I thought, aiding and abetting a criminal.

She brushed my hair away and touched my face. "It's hard to believe, but you're almost eighteen. You should have more of a say about things. You're right."

"That's all I'm saying."

She leaned back and I felt her weight shift the couch. "You know, I never told you this, but I had to go to the hospital for a little while when you were little. I was sleeping too much, that kind of thing. I guess I said some things I shouldn't have. Anyway, my mother committed me."

I sat up. "She *committed* you? Like to a mental hospital."

"That's where you commit people, right? It's why I don't talk to her anymore."

I'd wondered what had come between her and her family that had resulted in a complete lack of communication, but I'd never considered this. "That's the reason?"

She nodded. "The police came. I left you with her. What could I do? I went."

"I kind of remember it," I said. "Not you leaving, but other parts."

I had a sudden memory of my grandmother—the thick, gray stockings she used to wear, the clunky black shoes. The way her long, gray hair hung down in a thick braid I could pull from under the table.

"She hid me under the table and told me to knock on it and pretend to be a spirit," I said. "I kind of remember she used to pick people's pockets."

"She did," my mother said. "I'm sorry. It wasn't a great situation to leave you in."

"It's okay," I said. "You pick people's pockets, too."

"Just that once," she said. "I wanted to come back to you. I did. I was so weak, though. And young." She looked down at her hands. "The day she drove me back home, I remember thinking to myself, when I get to the house, when the car pulls up, I will not have the strength, I will just fall to the ground. I don't pray that often, but that day I did. I said, 'God, up there, I know you won't change my life or my financial situation because that is just the way that you are, but can you do this one little thing for me? Can you just please send me someone to help me get through all of this?' Something, I don't know what, made me look up at the window, right then, at that second. You know what I saw? You. You were partway behind the curtain. Your bangs were all uneven. My mother always cut bangs funny. Her own, too. I don't know if her eyesight was right. Your eyes were big and wide, like this." She opened her eyes as wide as possible and propped them apart with her fingers. "And your little nose was all smooshed up against the window. You looked so bright when you saw the car. Delighted. That was the word I thought of to describe you, *delighted*. It took so little back then to make you happy. You were just so happy just to see your mom."

I put my arms out to hug her in the dark.

"I'm always going to be there for you," I said.

She gripped my hand. "I know. And I'll always be there for you, too."

I don't think I could have said, right then, why we always fought so much. We were the Gemini twins, after all. The cattle thieves. Two halves of the same star cluster, stuck together for eternity. I loved her more than I'd ever loved anyone, but still, sometimes I wished it were different. I wished that our lives didn't feel so uncertain, so thrown up to the sky. I wished that our love didn't feel so much like a pact.

# TWENTY

Right after I made the decision to stay, business picked up. The Beverly Hills Hotel was a great place to work. There were rich people and movie stars everywhere; we only had to meet them. Joan introduced us to a few people at the hotel pool, and those people introduced us to their friends, and those to theirs. Within a week, we had twelve new clients. We didn't read cards anymore; we didn't have to. We marketed ourselves as mediums, and we bragged that we could communicate with anyone. Marilyn Monroe was in hot demand, as was Beethoven and also James Dean. There is no shortage of ghosts in Los Angeles, it seems. It's like anywhere else that way, though certainly, the dead are more glamorous, more eccentric. They speak to more people and are much better known.

"We're coming up in the world, Lindsey," my mother said. "We're better, different people," and I believed it. I believed we could be better and different, that money and a bit of success was all it took.

When Paco, Emily, and Scott came to the hotel, the first thing they said was, "You live here?"

I shrugged.

"And you get to use everything?" Emily asked. "The pool? All of it?"

"Pretty much," I said. She stepped ahead of me on the path and spun around. That's when I noticed she was carrying my purse.

"Did you buy that bag from Sydney?" I asked her.

"What, this?" she said. "Nah, she gave it to me. She said Mr. Aimes gave it back to her."

"She just gave it to you?" I said. It seemed like a trick to me.

Emily shrugged.

"Because you guys are friends now. Is that it?"

"It's just a purse, Lindsey."

"I know it's just a purse," I snapped.

Emily pushed the bag higher on her shoulder and walked ahead, leaving me a few steps behind. I looked at Paco for help, but he and Scott had their eyes down. Was I the only person who could see that Sydney just wanted to be close to Paco? That she was only pretending to be our friend?

I took a few quick steps and dropped back into place beside Emily.

"Wait, did she eat lunch with you today?" I truly didn't know. I'd missed the day due to a complaint from the hotel staff about a psychic table my mother had set up beside the pool. She'd been upset, and I'd been afraid she might argue with the concierge if I left her alone, so I'd had her call me in sick to school.

Emily didn't answer, which I decided was as good an answer as any.

We crossed to the pool and put our stuff down on a chair. Paco and Emily jumped in right away, but I hung back. I walked down the steps, an inch at a time, the way I always did. I liked to let my body adjust to the water, slowly. This way, it couldn't surprise me. I watched the others surface and thought, *Look at them, they've left me out.* Even though I knew it wasn't true.

"If you don't come in the next three seconds, we'll pull you in," Paco called out to me.

Scott sent a splash my way, then he turned around and put his arms around Emily. They were a couple, then. She'd told me at the party, but I'd forgotten. A week or two ago, I would have known. I would have paid enough attention to ask.

I was almost all the way in, so I ducked under. The water felt cold for a second, then exactly right. When I surfaced, Paco was beside me.

"I didn't even ask her about it," I gestured toward Emily. "I guess I haven't been the greatest friend."

"You've had stuff on your mind."

"True."

He looked back over at Scott. "People don't pick on him anymore. They're scared of her." He leaned back, treading water. "Hey, about the Sydney thing, you know I didn't tell her to sit with us, right?"

"I know," I said. "She told me she was going to."

"Just so we have that clear." He swam closer. "You know, I never really liked Sydney that much. I didn't feel the way about her that I feel about you."

It was the absolute best thing he could have said. We stood there, for a second or two, smiling at each other, then he dove down and took hold of my ankle. I struggled for a few seconds, but then I gave in. I let the water fill my ears and swallow me, and I let my body drop like a rock to the bottom of the pool. We stood on opposite sides of the drain, holding hands, until he said, "Let's go up."

I saw the words on his lips and read them, but I did not think I would leave, not yet. I shook my head. Paco looked panicked. He was running out of air, so I let go of his hands and watched him ascend. I looked up at the bottom of his feet, kicking, white soles in blue water, and then at the bubbles he left behind. I liked it there at the bottom of the pool. I liked the stillness of the water, the blank, blue light. I can hold my breath as long as I want, I told myself. I can stay here, in this warm, still, watery world, forever. But when I came up, I was breathing heavily. I was coughing and gasping for air.

I climbed out of the pool and started toward my towel, but halted when I noticed someone sitting in my chair. It was Willow, in a big straw hat. When she noticed me noticing her, she waved and lifted her margarita glass in the air.

"What's up?" Paco said when I returned.

"Nothing," I said. "I thought I saw someone I knew."

After everyone left, I sat down at one of the side tables to wait for Willow. The pool lights went on, turning the air aquamarine, and a white swirl of fog came to settle above the water. I shivered. I put my sweatshirt on over top of my wet suit, but it didn't do much to keep me warm. Fifteen minutes went by, then fifteen more. The night moved in, closer, and the temperature dropped. The pool glowed phosphorescent in the dark. I drew my bare knees up to my chest and slipped them under my sweatshirt.

"What darling little friends!" Willow's voice seemed to come from three directions at once. I looked to my left, and as I did, Willow popped out of a bush to my right. Like Rose and Maud, Willow had the habit of appearing and disappearing suddenly. None of them liked formalities, greetings, or farewells.

"Most people go to the hotel desk. They call us up," I said. I was irritated with her for startling me.

She laughed. "They do, do they? Well, I was just walking around. Checking on things. Where they keep security and all that."

"Oh," I said. I didn't know why she would need that information.

She sat down on the chair beside me and set her bag on the ground. Her shirt was wet where it stretched across her chest, and I could see the outline of her black striped bathing suit. The strong smell of chlorine swirled around her.

"So how are things going?" she asked. "Tell me every little detail."

"There's nothing to tell. We're just getting started."

She nodded. "You've got to build her trust. Do you want to swim? I'm thinking about taking a dip."

"No," I said. "You go ahead."

I leaned back in my chair and looked up. The crescent moon had the pale shape of a full moon behind it. An Old Moon in the arms of the new. A bad omen. I wished Willow would leave so I could take out my Moon Sign notebook and record it.

"Suit yourself." She walked over to the steps and started in. "I think this pool is warmer than the other one. You really should come in."

175

She treaded water across the pool until she was close to me again.

I stood up from my chair. "I'm going to walk back."

"Of course. Oh, and Lindsey."

"Yes?"

"Let us know when you two want to do a spirit circle."

"A spirit circle?"

"A séance. We usually do a séance at some point. A good séance has a way of flushing money out of people like nothing else. At a séance, you can ask for a donation on the table, so you always get something."

I wasn't sure I liked the idea of a séance. What did we know about putting on a séance? But I said, "Okay."

"Toodles," she said, and swam away.

When I got back to the hotel, I tried to tell my mother that I'd run into Willow, but she didn't want to talk or hear about it. A fresh silver dome of food stood in front of her, and she was too excited about it to care about much else. My mother had lost some weight recently. She didn't eat as much food, but she still ordered the same amount.

"It's a brand new thing," she said.

"Right," I said. It wasn't. We'd ordered everything in that hotel, but she always said it anyway. Sometimes, she'd clap her hands; she was *that* excited. But after a few initial exclamations, a few *ooh*s and *ahh*s, she only picked at the food. A couple bites, and she was on the phone again, ordering something else. I always waited until she finished, then I'd wrap up what was left and put it away. The refrigerator was filled to overflowing with my tinfoil packages.

"What on Earth is all this?" my mother asked once when she opened the fridge. She put her hand in tentatively and picked up a package from the top of the pile. "Why, it's the roast duck! From a week ago!" She wrapped the package back up, but the rotten meat smell remained in the room. "How far back does it all go? Wow! You've certainly done a job here! Have you been saving everything?"

"Not everything," I said. "Well, everything, I guess."

She looked up at me, astonished. "Why would you do this, Lindsey? Why?"

I wasn't sure, myself. Looking at it now, it seemed strange to me, too. It seemed like the work of someone else. "I didn't want to waste it," I said, finally. It wasn't really an answer; we were wasting it, just in a slower way, but it was the best answer I could manage.

"My promise to you is that from here on out, we'll always have enough to eat," she proclaimed.

"I know that," I said.

She put her hand on my shoulder before she turned away.

When I was a child, I used to hoard holiday candy: chocolate hearts and candy canes, cream eggs and those miniature Hershey bars that people hand out on Halloween. I'd save it for months, years sometimes, tucked away in an old shoebox at the back of my closet. I'm not sure why I did this. I don't remember being hungry. Not exactly. Not . . . extremely. Anyway, the thing I remember best is that when I finally got around to eating the candy, it was a big disappointment. Stale and dull and so hard I had to break some of it with a hammer. Chocolate, if left in a shoebox, will melt and harden until it takes on a new form. It will taste like syrup or cardboard or even dirt. Red Hots will not stay red and they will not stay hot, and candy hearts will crumble in your fingers. When I finally realized this, when I dumped the whole pile into the trash, I stood for a long time in front of it, still not ready to give it up. I had witnessed ruin with my own tongue, but I did not believe the truth: accumulation is worthless. And hoarding is just another form of waste.

# TWENTY-ONE

The following Monday, half the school was out with the flu. The sound of coughing filled the halls, and the air had the slushy, stuffed-nosed smell I'd always associated with winter, but that seemed wrong, here, in the bright L.A. sun.

"Scott threw up in biology," Sydney told me near my locker. "All over the place."

"That's sad," I said. I felt bad for kids who threw up in school. People always made fun of them.

"And funny," she said. "I thought Emily was going to get in a fight about it. Some guy was saying stuff, making stupid gagging noises, that type of thing, and she came flying out of nowhere and started slamming him with her purse. I don't think he knew what to do. He just kind of stood there while she hit him again and again." She picked up her backpack. "Hey, are you going to lunch?"

I was on my way to lunch, but I didn't want her to come. I nodded vaguely to dismiss her question.

"I think I'm getting sick," she said. She coughed twice and grabbed my arm. "Hey, you got a new uniform."

"I did," I said.

She put my arm down and grabbed my purse. "And a bag. What kind of bag is this? Where's that pleather thing?"

"I got some new stuff."

She sighed. "My stuff is such crap."

A UPS man walked toward us with a package for the office and I jumped. He had the exact same mustache as one of the officers who had shown up at the Sepulveda apartment, but when I looked again, I realized it wasn't him. I'd become paranoid lately. I was always seeing the police.

"Are you going to lunch or what?" Sydney asked.

She didn't wait for me to answer. She crossed the lawn ahead of me, her long legs moving like quick scissors beneath her short skirt. When she came to the spot where the others were, she sat down and smiled up at me like a magician. She'd just yanked my friends out from underneath me with a flick of her tablecloth, and I was alone now. The one rattling, remaining plate.

She took a bite of Paco's sandwich and said, "Hey, Lindsey, if you don't want to do the fortune-teller thing at the fundraiser, I'll do it. I'll even put my picture on the website. I don't care."

She knew about that? I looked over at Paco, who was looking very intently at something across the lawn. "I don't mind," I said.

"Lindsey's doing it," Paco said.

"Sure," Sydney said. "Of course she is. I just meant if she didn't want to do it is all."

She sprawled out on the grass, squinting at the courtyard with a bored expression on her face. After a while, she started up a conversation with Emily about makeup. Emily was taking a cosmetology class. She wanted to be a makeup artist someday, so they talked about that for a while, then they moved on to discuss hairstyles. They both liked short hair, but no shorter than a person's chin. That length was absolutely correct for everyone, even for men.

"Your hair, for instance, is all wrong," Sydney told Paco. He looked concerned. "It is?"

"It looks like someone went at it with a lawn mower," Emily said.

Sydney laughed and scooted up on Paco's lap to fix it. *Tell her to get off*, I thought, but he didn't. He sat very still and obedient while she adjusted his hair.

I waited until the others left for class, and then I told Paco, "It would be different if you didn't eat it up."

"What are you talking about?" he said.

"Sydney. The way she paws all over you. You like it."

"She doesn't paw all over me," he said.

"She does," I said. "And you allow it, and it makes me look bad, like a jealous person when I say anything. I hate it."

All around us, on every side, locker doors slammed.

"You're serious, aren't you?" He looked as surprised as if I had just plucked what I said out of the sky.

"Yes. Don't you see it?"

"I don't know," he said. "Give an example."

It seemed incomprehensible to me he needed one, that he could have missed any of it, but truly his face was blank. "Just go to class," I told him.

I didn't wait to see if he'd left. I sat down on the hallway floor and took out my Moon Sign notebook. I wrote Sydney's name and circled it as a declaration of war.

Her birthday was August 2. I could figure out her planets from that, but I'd have to look it up.

"What are you doing there?" Paco said.

"Just go to class," I said, again.

I thought he would go, but a minute later, when I looked up from my chart, he was still standing there, looking down at me.

"Give me this thing," he said. He pulled it from me and started to go through it. "What are all these lists stuffed in here? You make charts of the arguments you get into?"

"Give it back," I said. I tried to take it, but he held it out of my reach.

"Are these . . . Are they all about your mother?"

"Not all of them," I said. I'd written Sydney's name in it now, too. I looked down at the floor. The charts were stupid when I really thought about it.

"You record all this stuff?" he said. "You, like, save it in this? Forever?"

People crisscrossed between us, headed to class, but we stayed still.

"You can't hold on to things like that, Lindsey." He tossed it back to me and started walking backward in the direction of his next class.

"Yeah, yeah," I said. "Whatever." I looked down at the book. The last page had a tear at the corner, in the spot where I'd tried to grab it.

"Hey, I'm not anywhere in that Moon notebook, am I?" he said.

"No."

"Good," he said. He turned around and started down the hall.

After school that day, I walked into the bungalow and found a telescope next to the couch. I didn't recognize the brand, but I could tell from the size and the shape of the lens that it wasn't cheap. I looked at the room upside down through it, then I searched around for a card to indicate it might be for me. I didn't see one, but I decided to thank Joan, anyway.

I left the living room and walked into the kitchen. Joan was standing beside the counter, holding a baked potato up to the light.

"The telescope is great," I said.

She nodded, still looking at the potato. "Consider it a late Christmas gift. It's very strange, but I think someone has removed the toppings from this potato."

"I'm sorry," I said. "I don't know why she does that."

She lifted the domed lid off of the silver platter, and we both peered inside. My mother had taken small, moon-shaped bites out of pretty much everything.

"I'll order another plate, for you," I said. It had become my policy, now, to involve the hotel staff in the smallest details of our lives.

Joan waved the suggestion away. She picked up a cheese sandwich with a missing corner and popped it into her mouth, then she bent down to feed a half-eaten carrot to the rabbit. "She even got the ones I save for Houdini. Poor Houdini Weenie. A big bad human got your food." He stood up obediently on his hind legs to nibble it.

"I'm sorry," I said again.

She stared at me suspiciously. "Why do you keep apologizing for her? Are you her?"

She drew her bushy eyebrows into one straight line, studying me. It occurred to me that Joan might truly be trying to figure out if I was my mother. Ever since the day at the gas station when she'd dumped the bottle of dark hair dye on her head, we did look a bit alike. A few people had even asked if we were sisters, which pleased my mother beyond description.

"No," I said. "Of course not."

She sat down at the table and set a picture of Saul and herself on the placemat across from her. I thought the photo might be my signal to leave, that she meant to dine alone with it, but when I stood, she said, "Please don't go."

I sat back down and we both looked at the photo. They were young, maybe twenty-five, dressed up and sitting at a restaurant table, on an old-fashioned couch. Saul's hair didn't look as big and outdated as Joan's. It was just a little long, a little stragglier than how men wore their hair today, and I could tell, in spite of it, that he was very handsome. He had a cheerful jauntiness to his posture, to the way he slung his arm around Joan's shoulder, that I liked. With his head back and his mouth half open, he looked like the kind of person who could talk you into anything. I thought I might understand, now, how Joan had come to believe she would never be alone.

"Saul was an actor, right?"

She nodded. "Well, he was in that one film. He played Houdini. You know, the magician."

I hadn't seen the film, but I'd read about it online when we were researching her, so I nodded. I remembered something my mother told me that day. Saul had died more than a year ago, she said, but some people just don't cycle through grief in a normal way. I pictured Joan on a bicycle, hitting something sticky and tumbling off.

"He always felt he never really made it as an actor," she said. "It bothered him that I had to support us both. I would have built up my career anyway, though. And he balanced me. You should always try to have someone in your life who can pull a rabbit from a hat."

"I'll try to remember that," I said.

She nodded. "The other day, I smelled his aftershave on someone. You know, I think I may have genuinely scared that man."

For a second, I considered asking what the aftershave was, so we could spray it around at the séance. I felt disgusted with myself for even thinking of it.

Joan picked up the picture of Saul and touched his face. "I know he's gone, but sometimes I just wish I could see him one more time."

I could have searched forever, through every available word and sentence, and not found a single thing to say that might help her. And I liked Joan. I truly did.

"Your mother says it's possible," she said.

"Maybe it is," I said. I looked down at her face, reflecting back at us from the silver platter, and thought that she looked a bit like John the Baptist with his head on a plate. Out of all the stories I'd heard at school, that one bothered me the most. It was the blood, I suppose, the Halloween freak show nature of the severed head. But also, I think, it was the dancing girl. How did she feel, I wondered, when the music stopped? When she'd danced her dance and charmed the king and gained her wish. And her mother leaned in and told her to ask for the head.

185

"Thank you," Joan said, although I couldn't think of anything I'd said or done worth the gratitude. In reality, I should have been thanking her, every day, for everything she was doing for us. She seemed lost, temporarily, to the material world, but then she must have remembered her role as my mentor because she looked up very suddenly and said, "So!"

"Yes?" I asked.

"How about you? How is school going?"

"Okay, I guess."

She struck a spoon against the silver platter. "I don't like that principal. A real butt kisser, that lady."

"She's okay," I said.

She lowered her glasses on her nose, the way the principal did, and we both laughed. For a while after that, we didn't say anything. She just nibbled the edge of a cracker. Then she said, "Okay, so what's really bothering you?"

Her question surprised me. I'd assumed she was too preoccupied, both with Saul and the potato, to get a good reading of my mood. "I had sort of a fight with Paco at lunch."

"Well, you have to expect that," she said.

"You do?"

She nodded. "You're getting ready to leave for school next year. People who care about each other always fight just before a separation."

"They do?" I asked. That didn't make sense to me. UCSC was only a few hours away. Paco and I had talked about it, about how we'd drive back and forth on the weekends if I was accepted.

"I think it's more because of this girl," I said.

I told her about Sydney. When I finished, she said, "Hmm. Well, how does he act toward her?"

"Not that interested," I admitted.

She nodded, thinking this over. "Well, there you go."

"So you're saying I should trust him?" I said.

She looked surprised. "How would I know if he's trustworthy?"

She walked over to the trashcan and dumped the rest of the potato in. Then she paused thoughtfully over the swinging lid. "Did I tell you that I let Houdini go once?"

"No," I said.

"It was during the mudslide. The authorities called me on the phone. They told me I was going to die if I didn't leave right away. Anyway, after I hung up, I was so depressed I was actually okay with it. I thought, I'll just slide down the hill a little with the house, see what comes of it. But then I realized I couldn't in good conscience make that decision for Houdini, so I opened the door and threw him out."

"You threw him out into the rain?"

"Well, I didn't have many options. I said to him, 'It's time, now, Houdini, for you to live an outdoor life. Go find a cozy little rabbit hole. Mommy is saving your life.'"

I thought I could see where she was going with it.

"And he came back," I said. "You loved him and set him free and he came back."

"No, he hopped into a giant flowerpot and got stuck. When I realized the house had slid all it was going to, I scooped him up and brought him back in."

"So," I said, "the moral is . . . to let go?" I still had the idea that there might be a way to understand the story.

She turned away from me, and looked out the window sideways, like a passenger on a train. "Correct."

"You might need to let go a little, too, Joan," I said, but I don't think she heard me. She was still looking out the window when I left.

When the sun went down that evening, I dragged the telescope out to the patio and aimed it up at the sky. It steadied me to see the North Star, Cassiopia, and all the constellations in their predictable spots, like points on a map. I searched for Jupiter, found it, and brought the lens down. The January Wolf Moon was rising, prowling the towers of the pink hotel. I took out my Moon Sign notebook and wrote:

*Full Wolf Moon. Tooth marked and thin. It looks like it wouldn't think anything of swallowing the entire sky.*

# TWENTY-TWO

We spent the rest of the winter at the hotel while work progressed on Joan's house.

"Sometimes I think I don't care if it ever gets built," Joan said one night, while she and my mother were looking over the plans.

"It's going to be a fabulous house," my mother said. "Look at your pool here. Is that a tennis court?"

"Yes. I wonder if I should have put it in. If I'll use it."

"Lindsey plays tennis," my mother said.

Joan brightened. "Do you play tennis?" she asked me.

I looked up from my homework. "No, but I'd like to learn."

"What are you studying over there?" she asked.

"Calculus."

"Let me know if you need any help."

"Okay," I said, "thanks."

"Or I can help," my mother added. "I'm pretty good at math."

"This is calculus," I said, and instantly felt bad. I knew she wished she'd done better at school.

On the night of the fundraiser carnival for the playground, I brought my costume back to the hotel, unzipped it from its plastic bag, and laid it out on my mother's bed. I traced my fingers along the glittery neckline and over the pearl-shaped buttons on the sleeves, then I turned it over. Someone had spilled ink on the back. The stain stretched from the top of the zipper all the way down to the glitter sash waist.

"It had to have been one of the South Node Ladies who did it," my mother said when I showed it to her. "Maud maybe. No, probably Willow."

"The South Node Ladies snuck into the school so they could spill ink on a costume they didn't know I was going to wear?"

"I think so," she said. "Yes."

She walked over to the dresser, picked up a bottle of perfume, and sprayed it. The cheerful, citrus-smelling cloud struck me, immediately, as false: a shopping mall scent, a scent on a card. You might smell it before you tossed it out, but it lacked some warm, human quality that might make you buy it.

She took a long sniff. "What do you think of this scent?"

"I actually like your patchouli better," I said.

She looked pleased and surprised. "Me, too. I bought this to give to Joan. Do you think she'll like it?"

"I don't know." I looked back at the costume. "Can you believe this?"

"I can," she said. "If you knew even half the things those women have been up to."

My personal opinion was that Sydney had wrecked the costume. It just would have been easier for her to get into the school, but I didn't bring it up. I was too curious as to what else the South Node Ladies had been doing. "What do you mean?" I asked.

"Well, Maud's been soliciting her own checks in secret. She knocked on the door the other day. Said she was from another spiritualist church. And I caught Willow yesterday, walking around in a maid uniform."

"Willow was in a maid uniform?"

She put down the perfume. "I think she means to just steal Joan's things. I told you all of this, already."

My mother was always thinking she'd told me something she'd never actually mentioned.

"No," I said. "I would remember that." I imagined Willow in our room, among our things, picking them up, pretending to clean. It seemed worse than invasive. I would never sleep well in the hotel again.

My mother shrugged. "Well, now you know."

I nodded. In a way, it didn't surprise me. I'd always known we couldn't trust any of them, least of all Willow.

"Be home by ten, okay? We're having a planning meeting for Joan's séance with the South Node Ladies." She started for the door.

"Ten?" I asked.

"I told you about this, too."

"You didn't," I said. "Why don't you just go to the meeting and fill me in?"

She shook her head. "That'll be three against one. It'll be all uneven."

"You'll be okay," I told her. "You can be like three women when you want to be." I meant it to be flattering, but she frowned.

"Just be home at ten," she said. "I'm serious about this, Lindsey. Just do it."

She walked out the door and turned the television on in the next room, but I stayed. I sat on the bed and ran my finger along the stain on the costume. In this light, it formed a flattened-out purple question mark.

Who is honest? Who can I trust?

And who can trust me?

The carnival was in the parking lot of the school, and also inside, in the lobby. A dozen or so booths with dangling stuffed animal prizes circled a large kiddie pool full of floating plastic ducks. The fortune booth was off to the side of that—a small, purple tent. I expected it to be empty, but there was Sydney, sitting at the card table with her legs crossed, her hands moving like flapping birds over what was to be *my* crystal ball. Even in the dark, I could see that she was wearing the exact same costume (minus the stain) that I was.

I looked around for Paco. I spotted him in front of the lollipop tree and grabbed his arm.

"What's *she* doing?" I asked.

He shrugged. "I knew you would come up to me and say that. Exactly that."

"You knew right," I said. "There can't be two psychic readers."

He spun the lollipop tree around and looked up. "Why not? That's how your mother and you do it, right?"

"Right," I said. "And that's the whole problem with it. That's the reason I hate it."

He sighed. "I don't know why she sat there, Lindsey, but can you guys work it out? The dunking booth is broken.

Someone stole the raffle prize. I have a list, here, of about twelve problems to get to."

"Someone stole the raffle prize?"

He shrugged.

"I can work it out," I said. "But then you can't complain about how I do it."

"Deal," he said.

He walked away, and I looked back at Sydney. She was standing now, spreading my tarot cards on a table that looked a lot like the one we'd used in Oregon. I had to admit, she did it pretty well. If things were reversed, if I'd lived her life and she'd lived mine, she might have been a better daughter to my mother than I would ever, in a million years, be.

I walked up to the table, fully intending to kick her out, but at the last second, I changed my mind. I thought about what Joan had said about letting go of things, and it seemed true. If Sydney was willing to do the psychic table for me, it could actually be a good thing. It would give me time off, a vacation day. Why would I choose to work? I changed out of my costume and joined Emily and Scott at the bowling booth.

"Why aren't you at your booth?" Emily said. She offered me some of her popcorn but I shook my head. When I didn't take it, she leaned over to hand-feed it to Scott.

"Sydney kind of took care of it for me."

Emily looked across the room at her. "Want me to help you kick her out?"

"Nah," I said.

"You looked kind of stupid in the costume, anyway," she said.

I nodded. I'd thought so too.

"It was like it wasn't you."

"The thing is, it was, though. It's really my actual job."

"I know," she said. "That's the funny part about it."

I stayed with Emily and Scott at the bowling booth for the rest of the carnival, but I guess it must have looked like I wasn't doing much because the principal noticed me. She walked up in her clown nose and her big clown feet and told me that being a third person at a two-person booth wasn't something she considered work, and she signed me up for the clean-up crew. I had to stay behind at the end of the night, vacuuming and pulling gum off the dunking booth, while everyone else went to the after-carnival-party at the class president's house in Culver City. Still, I preferred it. It felt a lot less like work to me than sitting at the booth would have.

When I arrived at the party, Emily, Paco, and Scott were sitting on the lawn beside a wide, flowering shrub. They looked just as they did in school, set apart from everyone else in a tight, chatty circle.

"I probably didn't work it out the way you hoped," I told Paco. "I know you wanted me to do it."

I heard laughter and turned. Sydney was walking toward us with her bracelets jangling, her hips swinging beneath her glitter sash belt. I'd thought she was wearing the exact same fortune-teller costume I'd planned to wear that night, but now, up close, I could see the subtle differences. The skirt was shorter, and she had pulled the top down a good amount. As I looked her over, she staggered forward, tripped over a tower of beer cans, and threw up into a cactus plant.

"She needs to go home," Emily said. She knelt down in the dirt beside her and tried to pull back her hair.

"Shows what you know," Sydney said, except it came out, "Slows what you know."

"Who can still drive? Who can take her home?" Emily asked.

"I can," I said. I'd just gotten there. I hadn't had anything to drink. I looked down at my watch. It was already eleven. I was supposed to be home an hour ago, anyway, for the meeting. It would be easy for me to drop her off on the way.

"No," Sydney said. "Not you. Someone else." She rolled over on the ground and rested her head on Paco's lap.

Paco must have seen something in my eyes. He must have realized, finally, that this was the kind of thing I'd been complaining to him about, because he shifted back all of a sudden and her head fell to the grass. I was starting to feel sorry for her now. Her head had hit the ground pretty hard. And she had, after all, saved me from a night of psychic reading.

"That's very flattering," I told her, "but it has to be me."

Emily and I struggled to raise her to a standing position. It was harder than I expected. She weighed more than she looked like she weighed, and she was fighting us. She kicked my knee and one of her ankle bracelets snapped off. For a while, she cursed about that, but then she turned her attention to Paco.

"Come with us, Paco," she called as we led her away.

Emily told me Sydney's address, and we dumped her in the front seat of the car. I fastened her seat belt and said, "Don't throw up in the car."

"I have a stomach of steel," she said. Then she leaned out the window and puked some more.

I turned the radio on for noise and rolled down my window. The wind blew Sydney's hair out of her face, and I could see she was crying. I looked away from her, out the front window at the passing road.

"Where are you taking me?" she asked after a while.

"Where do you think?"

"Home?"

"That's right."

"No way," she said, suddenly alert. "Can't go there. My mother thinks I'm in my room right now."

"Mine's mad because I'm not at a meeting. You'll have to figure something out." I glanced down at the clock in the car. This was taking a lot longer than I'd expected. I tried not to imagine exactly how angry my mother was going to be, but an image of her face kept popping up on the dashboard in front of me.

Sydney leaned against the window. When she spoke, it was in a thin, slurred voice, like a song. "You're so lucky, Lindsey. You're so pretty. You have such a great boyfriend."

I turned, surprised, to look at her. She looked good— like a movie star in an action movie. Her hair was ruined, her dress ripped, but she still had her makeup on. She was still wearing sky-high heels, despite the bridge she had just jumped over and the mountain she had climbed.

"You're pretty," I told her.

"I'm not," she said, "even with the surgery, I'm not."

I looked at her again. I hadn't noticed she'd had any surgery. I decided that meant it must have gone well.

"It looks good. You look good." I said it in a casual tone. *I am a true resident of Los Angeles, now*, I thought. I can discuss plastic surgery with the rest of them.

She laughed. "My boobs are okay."

"Well, that's something," I said.

"I guess." She pointed to a white stone house and said, "That one."

I stopped the car. "Why do you do the things you do? I mean, you're fine. You could have friends."

She opened the door and rolled out onto the grass. A second later, she popped up again in the passenger side window. "I guess I just want the whole stupid world."

She staggered up the front walk. A light went on, and a very tiny, blond woman who must have been her mother appeared, like a cuckoo from a clock. Sydney towered over her. Yet, when Sydney fell, her mother managed to pick her up and kick the door back open with one foot.

*This is how normal girls apologize to their mothers*, I thought. They stumble toward them blind, smeared in lipstick, stinking of beer and boys and whatever dark night they've just come in from. They fall down on top of them, and they wait for their mothers to forgive them enough to carry them home.

# TWENTY-THREE

When I got back to the hotel, the first thing I said to my mother was: "I'm sorry."

"I specifically told you," she said, "to be home by ten. What part of *ten* did you not understand?"

Joan looked up from her seat on the couch. "Where were you two off to, anyway? What was so dang important about ten o'clock tonight?"

My mother pressed her lips together. She couldn't mention the meeting in front of Joan, which meant she couldn't speak, which was always very hard for her.

"Give her a break," Joan said. "She's in love. Remember love?"

"Vaguely," my mother said. "Love or not, she needs to learn to be where she's supposed to be. Used to be you didn't have to tell her that. Used to be she knew."

"Maybe she does," Joan said thoughtfully. "Have you ever thought that maybe she is exactly where she's supposed to be?"

I looked over at Joan and thanked her silently.

"When I was her age," Joan said. "I followed the Grateful Dead around for an entire summer. My mother freaked out. She was sure I would end up drugged and dead on the street."

I thought about Joan, younger, with longer hair, no job, and no possessions but the tie-dyed shirt she wore. It fit, somehow.

"Teenagers are hard on their mothers," my mother said. "It's the sad, awful truth."

"What were you doing at her age?" Joan asked.

"I was in upstate New York," my mother said. She leaned out the window and tried to pluck one of the night blooming flowers that grew along the side of the bungalow. She never could just look at things. She had to take them. "At Audrey Way. My mother was a medium there."

"And now you're a medium," Joan said. "Just like your mother. What did you say her mother was before that?"

"A fortune-teller." She looked up at the ceiling as if she'd just heard something, and I thought that maybe I'd heard it, too—the whispers of all of those women before us.

"It's a sad fact that we all turn into our mothers," Joan said.

In the corner of the room, my heart skipped a beat. If what she'd said was true, I might only have a short time left.

Although she'd sworn it would not be possible, my mother was able to reschedule the meeting with the South Node Ladies for the next Saturday afternoon. It turned out I was almost late for the make-up meeting, too, because Saturday was the day I went to the Sepulveda apartment to get our mail. I'd been waiting for my letter from UCSC, so I was usually pretty good about checking it, but I'd missed a week, so today, the box was crammed full. When I opened it, everything spilled out, and some flyers blew into a rose bush. I let them go, because shoved in the back, was a very large envelope from UCSC.

A large envelope is a good sign, but I still wasn't sure. I carried it up to Paco's apartment and rung the bell. A few seconds passed, and he appeared in pajama pants.

"What's it say?" he asked. He walked out to the balcony and shut the door behind him.

"I don't know. I didn't open it."

"Do you want me to?"

I always felt it was worse to hear bad news from someone else, so I said no.

"Just rip it," he said. "Go."

I opened it and slid the letter out, but I had to read it three times to understand it.

"I got in," I said.

"You got in!" he repeated. He picked me up and swung me around in a circle. We spun and cheered until we knocked over a chair and a tricycle and a potted plant. Then we stared at the destruction and laughed.

I had to run two red lights to make the meeting, and I was still five minutes late. My mother was frowning when I pulled up to the hotel, but when I told her about UCSC, she forgot to be mad. She had tears in her eyes when she hugged me.

"This is my college girl," she shouted to the others. "Hey, look at my college girl."

The South Node Ladies called out their congratualations from the sidewalk, but I could see that they actually didn't care. Maud and Rose barely looked up, and Willow was fumbling with her purse. They moved closer together and waited for us to walk over.

My mother called the meeting to order. She took a step back to make it clear that she was the speaker and we were the audience, but then, just before she began, something stopped her. On the palm tree to her left, two flyers hung crookedly, one over the top of the other. "Who put this here?" she asked.

She pulled the top flyer down and crumpled it in her hand. Her flyer was visible, now, although a large foot-shaped mud mark obscured the top. At the bottom, across the top of the smiling caricature my mother had drawn of herself, someone had made their own marks in thick blue pen. My mother had a penis now, a big one, as well as a beard and a mustache.

"Would you look at that?" my mother said. "It's a penis. Did one of you do this?"

"Now, why would any of us do that?" Rose said. "Try to think logically, Debbie. Why would one of us draw a penis on you?"

My mother held the flyer up and to the side, viewing it all from another angle: the new frown, the startled eyes, the surprising blue tufts of facial and pubic hair.

"I always wondered how I'd look as a man," she said. "A little bit like Abe Lincoln, I think. I like it. Honest Abe."

I raised my hand to pull the flyer down.

"Leave it," my mother said.

"But it's a penis!" Rose said.

"You should take it down," Willow said. "That's my opinion."

"It will stay where it is," my mother said, "until one of you admits to drawing it."

She launched into a long explanation of the many ways she didn't trust any of them. She talked about catching Willow in a maid uniform and spotting Maud soliciting at the door. She accused them all, as a group, of throwing ink at my costume.

"You've made some pretty big charges, here, Debbie," Maud said. "Lindsey, do you agree?"

"Yes," I said. I had no idea if what she was saying was true, but I felt like I should defend her. I didn't like the way they were ganging up on her. "Except for the ink thing. I'm pretty sure that was someone else."

The South Node Ladies took their turns next. They accused me and my mother of actions that ranged from complete and all-out sabotage of our plan to defraud Joan to stealing crystal necklaces off the rearview mirrors of their cars. It might have gone on forever if Maud hadn't held up her hands to silence everyone.

"That's enough," she said.

We all agreed we would need to unite if we were to pull off the scam with Joan.

Willow said, "Debbie, has Joan told you any more about what she wants?"

"She's asked for a physical séance," she said. "Flying trumpets, all that." A car went by and her jacket billowed up.

"It's old-fashioned," Maud said. "No one does it anymore."

"For good reason," Rose said.

"What's a physical séance?" I asked.

My mother sighed. "It's like a normal séance, but you have to supply physical proof. The spirits have to appear or speak or throw things or fly trumpets in the air."

"What on Earth were you thinking, Debbie, when you agreed?" Willow asked.

"It's not her fault," I said, although I wasn't sure. It probably was her fault, but I didn't like the way Willow was talking to her. I remembered Joan the other night, saying something about mediums flying trumpets in Saul's Houdini movie. "You three don't know Joan. When she gets something in her head, you can't get it out."

My mother nodded, and we exchanged a confiding look. We were a team again, and it felt good. It felt as familiar as the lines on my palm.

"My point exactly," she said. She waved her hand in the air in the secret signal we had for "well done," and turned to face the others.

"I'll order the trumpets," Rose said.

"Wait on that," Maud said. "I might be able to get them from my sister."

"We might not have time to wait," my mother said. "That's the other thing. Joan's spent a lot on her house this month and on the hotel. And the real estate market's down. She's lost some money on her investments."

"Joan is running out of money?" I asked.

"I don't know if she's running out," my mother said, "but she's lost some, yes."

# TWENTY-FOUR

I was standing beside my locker when Emily showed me the letter.

"It's Scott's," she said.

"What does it say?" I could tell from her voice that something was wrong.

She handed it to me, but before I could read it she said, "The school lost a donor. They're discontinuing the scholarships."

I felt the hallway lurch beneath me. I had a sudden memory of Joan in her fuzzy pink bathrobe and slippers, strolling around the kitchen with a cocktail tray full of charity requests. I'd seen a pink ribbon, a red dress sticker, and the face of the sad little puppy on the Humane Society envelope twirl into the trashcan just before she slammed the lid.

I thought back to the meeting, to what my mother had said about Joan having lost money over the last few months. She must have been getting ready for the séance. She must have noticed her money dwindling and pulled it from the school. Why hadn't I seen it coming? We'd provided her with an alternate church, after all. Who donates to two churches?

"It starts next year," Emily said. "It won't affect us. Just Scott and Paco."

Paco and Scott were juniors. They would have to switch schools. Joan had thought of me, then, when she made her decision. Somehow, it made it worse. It made me the worst person in the world.

"Can you talk to her?" Emily asked. "I mean, you live with her, right?"

I considered it. I could tell Joan the Gone But Not Forgotten Spiritualist Church was a sham, and that she should keep giving her money to the school, which actually helped people. But she could call the police and turn us in. Also, Joan had already dropped the school. There was no guarantee, even if I told her everything, that she would decide to rejoin her old church.

"It wouldn't matter." I handed her back the letter and she took it. She looked disappointed, but not surprised.

"You're probably right," she said.

The bell rang, and she left. I watched her walk down the hall until I could only see the ponytail at the top of her head. After a while, Scott's head appeared beside hers. He held up a hand to wave to me before they both turned into the band room.

It's so much easier when you don't care about people. My mother knew this all along. Why had it taken me so long to figure it out?

After class, I met Paco at the top of the hill. I couldn't see his face well because of the sun, but his voice had an edge to it I didn't like.

"Emily said you were upset," he said.

"I'm okay."

His shadow shifted on the grass. "You heard about the scholarships, huh?"

I nodded.

"It's crazy, huh?"

"Yeah."

I looked down the hill, at the shoddy vegetable garden the kids in the other building had planted. Some of the kids wouldn't get the chance to see it grow. No one would play on the Saul Fields playground that stood half built to the right of it. This is a charity, I thought. Whatever anyone thinks about these people or what they believe, they have good intentions. They don't give donated money to themselves.

Paco must have seen me look at the playground because he said, "We have the carnival money, but it didn't work out to be all that much. It won't cover what we need to finish building it."

I felt terrible, and something about feeling terrible made me lash out at him. "It's just a playground. It's not like someone died or something."

"No," he said carefully. "It's not. You know what? You're in a really bad mood." He said this in a very accusing way. He said it like my mood was the very worst thing imaginable, when my bad mood, actually, was only a tiny part of what was wrong.

"You're acting weird," he said. "Are you trying to break up with me?"

I didn't realize it until he said it, but then, instantly, I knew it was the only option. How could I stay with him and at the same time do this to him?

I nodded.

He looked surprised. That was the worst part, how surprised he looked. I wanted to tell him I hadn't meant it. I wanted to put my head on his chest and wrap my arms around him, but I stood still.

"Okay," he said. "I get it."

He didn't get it. He didn't get anything, but I didn't say anything else. I watched him disappear back into the school, then I looked down the hill. The wind was blowing. Cars were going by. I sat down on the hard clay ground and put my head down on my knees. After a while, I pulled out the take-home calculus test I was supposed to complete that night, crumpled it up and threw it against the wall. Later, I thought, I will remember this day as a failing test. The day I sat up on this hill like a mad mathematician, unsolving equations, and subtracting everything in my life that mattered to me.

After that, I still had to make it through lunch. I walked out to the courtyard and sat down by myself in my old spot beneath the Eucalyptus tree. I spread my lunch out on the familiar flat rock and ate in silence. After a while, I opened my history book and tried to read, but I wasn't in the mood to care much about the past. I took out my tarot deck and picked up the first card. The Hermit, I guessed, but when I turned it over, I saw the Hanged Man.

After a while, Emily walked over. "Why aren't you sitting with us?" she demanded.

I remembered, suddenly, the day (it seemed so long ago now) that she'd made me promise I'd still sit with her if I broke up with Paco.

"I can't," I said. "I'm sorry."

"I'll sit here then. Girls stick together, right?"

"Right," I said.

"Was it because of Sydney?"

"What?" I was too distracted to really pay attention to her.

"You and Paco. The reason you broke up. Because she tried to kiss him?"

"She tried to kiss him?"

"She did, but he pushed her away."

It didn't matter now, but still, I was glad to hear it.

Emily crossed her legs. "You look like crap, you know. You look like you've been crying for two days."

I had cried a little bit, out behind the school after Paco left, but I thought I'd cleaned myself up. Apparently not. "Thanks," I said.

"I might be able to fix it with some concealer. I've got a new one. It looks kind of green till you put it on, but it works really well."

She reached inside her purse and took out a small compact and a flat brush.

"It's okay," I said.

"It's not, really. You should see yourself."

She squirted something out of a tube and dabbed it under my eyes.

"See, look at my eyes," she said. "It works. I've been crying nonstop about the scholarship thing all day. You really need a lot of product. Wow! I've never used so much product on someone's eyes."

"I don't really want to talk about the scholarships anymore," I said. I also didn't want to talk about my eyes, but I didn't mention that.

"Okay," she said, but by the way she looked at the ground, I could tell she was hurt that I didn't want to talk to her. I should never have made friends here. My mother was right.

"I think you should eat with Scott and Paco," I told her. "I really just want to be by myself."

Then she was gone. I'd lost my very last friend.

When I got back to the hotel, Joan and my mother were sitting in the living room. Joan was pacing the floor, wringing her hands, while my mother knelt at the coffee table in front of her, pretending to practice for the séance. Lately, she'd spent a lot of time researching the best way to train. She'd checked out a book on the subject, and she'd sent away for a pamphlet titled "Physical Mediumship, The Next Logical Step." For a while she had an Internet chat going with an elderly spiritualist medium who claimed she knew how to mix up ectoplasm and fly trumpets. My mother must have realized, at some point, that she didn't have the necessary skill or the patience to actually do any of the things she had learned because she'd resorted to tricking Joan with refrigerator magnets. She had one in her hand now, wrapped up in crumpled paper, and she was moving a bigger one beneath it, under the table in the leg of her pants.

Joan wasn't watching the training carefully; I decided that was probably a good thing.

"It's getting exciting," she said when she saw me, but really, she didn't look excited. She smiled up at me with such a terrible, sorrowful expression on her face that it hurt physically to look at her.

*I'm sorry*, I thought. *I'm so sorry, Joan.* I said it so loudly in my mind that Joan must have heard it because she said, "What?"

I grabbed my purse and walked outside. I didn't know where I was going, and pretty soon I realized I wasn't going anywhere because I had grabbed my mother's purse by mistake. I picked her things out of it one by one and threw them down on the ground. It felt good to do this small, mean thing. I watched her hair brush bounce to the grass and her compact smash against a rock. I felt more and more satisfied with each item I threw. When OUR LIST OF THINGS FOR A BETTER LIFE fell out, I laughed aloud at it. Then I threw it in the fountain.

It floated like a paper boat. It spun in a circle, then tipped, then dove beneath a stream of rushing water. I watched it bob up and down and finally sink, thinking the whole time that I didn't need it anymore. The funny thing about that list is that the whole time I was writing it, I already had a good enough life. I just didn't recognize it. Both were gone now, the paper and the good life. Later, when I thought about that list, down at the bottom of the Beverly Hills Hotel fountain, with all of those pennies and thrown away wishes, I thought that I'd picked an appropriate place to put it to rest.

I didn't go back to school the next day, or the day after that, but I pretended to. I left earlier than I ever did for class, and I returned later. I took to standing outside of 7-Eleven, dining on bottles of soda and chili dogs wrapped in silver paper, and to sitting for long periods on benches at bus stops. When the Big Blue Bus came, I'd board it. I never asked where it was going. I'd ride around in whatever great loop it took me in. *I'm leaving,* I'd think. *I'm starting my own life. The only one thing I have to do is pick a stop and get off.* I saw most of Santa Monica this way, and some of Culver City. I saw the main strip of Hollywood, lit at dusk, but I never did manage to step off that bus.

When night came, the view was always the same: my face, thinner than I remembered it, and tired. I'd gaze past it, searching for the next stop, the one that would bring me back to the hotel. Back to Joan. Because whatever loop I took, it always came around to her. It's a terrible thing to decide to ruin someone financially. But, you see . . . regardless of what I decided to do, *someone* was going to be ruined financially. If it wasn't Joan, it would be my mother. It was an improbable seesaw, but a seesaw nonetheless. And I didn't want to be the thing that upset the balance and knocked someone off.

# TWENTY-FIVE

We hadn't heard from the South Node Ladies, so I called Maud on the phone.

"We need to move this thing forward," I said. I still didn't know what I wanted to do—who was I supposed to protect? Joan or my mother?—but I knew we couldn't drag it out. My mother had told me that the South Node Ladies were still waiting for the trumpets they meant to fly at the séance.

"Lindsey?" Maud's voice sounded large on the other end, self-righteous. "Are you at the hotel?"

"Yes. Well, I'm outside of it. I'm on my cell phone."

"A cell phone!" She clucked her tongue. "Well, that doesn't sound safe. No, it doesn't." There had been a botched faith healing at the church a month before. It had drawn some news coverage, and reporters were still sniffing around. Maud was still nervous about it. "Let's do this. I want you to meet me, okay? Can you get to the church? Take the hotel limo or a cab or something. I'll give you the fare when you get here. Can you do that?"

"Okay," I said.

"Now, I'm going to ask you one more thing and I need you to answer it truthfully. Is your mother there with you now? Just say yes or no."

"No," I said. Actually, she was. Actually, she had her ear pressed against the back of the phone. When she heard what Maud said, she pressed even harder, and I had to take a step sideways to keep from falling over.

"Good, good, good," Maud said. "That will certainly make things easier. Make something up then, and come tonight, okay? We'd like to talk to you. All of us would."

I walked out to the front of the hotel and stood on the red carpet while the valet called a cab. The driver who pulled up was somewhere in his twenties, with long hair in a ponytail and a bright tie-dyed shirt. A string of rosary beads jangled on his rearview mirror.

"Where to?" he asked.

I told him the address and waited while he plugged it into his navigation system.

"Sketchy area," he said. He looked me over, again, in the rearview mirror. "Whole different place than the Beverly Hills Hotel."

He tried to make small talk, but my heart wasn't in it, so I kept my answers short. When he started driving, I leaned against the window and looked out at passing cars. Twice, I thought I saw Paco's blue Ford, and once I thought I saw Paco. He appeared, leaning out the passenger side window of an old red truck, in a white T-shirt and a black leather jacket.

The man I thought might be Paco moved closer, until suddenly he wasn't Paco anymore. He was just a regular man, a stranger, some type of Hell's Angel by his jacket but unremarkable in every other way. My heart lurched after him as he rolled away.

The church was small, almost windowless, the color of dirty snow. It had a flat roof, a tiny rectangular garden, and a narrow row of steps that led up to a plain brown door. In truth, it looked more like a house than a church. If it hadn't had a small, white garden sign in front of it that said, THE GONE BUT NOT FORGOTTEN SPIRITUALIST CHURCH, I might not have known I'd found it.

I walked up the lit path. The cab idled outside for a second. The driver must have thought twice about letting me off in this place in the dark, but then someone honked and he moved on. I waved to him as he pulled out. I meant it to look confident, but the motion came out choppy and uncertain.

When the cab drove off, I surveyed the street. I seemed to be in a residential area. That is, the other buildings beside the church looked like houses, much as the church did, although these structures clearly were homes. The house next to the church had a metal swing set outside, and the one across from it had three plastic chairs and a couch on its porch.

When I knocked on the door, the curtain in the front window rustled. I thought I saw someone peek out, but when no one appeared, I let myself in. I opened the door into what must have at one time been a parlor of sorts. In most ways, it still looked like one. Two fat purple couches faced an aged wood table, and a piano stood to one side. A long, two-way mirror covered one wall.

"Hello," I called. When no one answered, I started down the hall, past a paper-strewn office and toward the open door. This spot, which was likely meant to be a master bedroom, was now a makeshift sanctuary. Rows of folding chairs stood in front of a cloth-covered table, and various pictures of mediums hung on the wall. I looked down the long row and wondered which ones believed in what they were doing and which ones were frauds like us. It seemed impossible to pick between them. The Fox Sisters, the ones who started it all, stared blankly out at the proceeding generations.

I stepped into the sanctuary, and an organ started up. A slow hymn, mixed with what sounded like the call of a whale. Rose, Willow, and Maud were sitting in a line in the front row, facing the pulpit. I stopped in the aisle beside them, and they moved over to make room.

"Lindsey," Rose said. She meant it as a greeting, I think, but it came out as more of an announcement. Her hands gripped the handle of her lunchbox-shaped purse.

Maud spoke next. "I'm glad you called because I have something to tell you. There's no easy way to say this. . . ."

"We're worried about your mother," Willow said.

"She's making things up," Rose said.

"She's accused us of all sorts of things," Maud added.

"She's delusional!" Rose said.

They were speaking so fast, one on the tail of the other, that it made my head spin. I watched the keys of the self-playing piano move up and down and tried to sort it all out.

"She's not delusional," I said. "She just gets mixed up."

Maud shook her head. "It's hard for you to see it."

"It's because the north node of the moon was in Virgo when you were born," Rose said. "With a south node in Pisces, you have trouble sorting truth from illusion."

"An unfortunate chart," Willow said. "Not much she can do about it."

"It's her fate," Rose said.

215

"She can't relax into her south node like we can," Maud said. "Not with a node like that. Too much trouble for her if she does. Too much trouble for her mother."

"Just stop," I said. "All of you."

I didn't want to talk about the nodes of the moon. It just did not seem like a sufficient enough concept to explain the vast sky of confusion that existed between me and my mother.

"If you spout off enough astrology, eventually you'll hit on something."

Rose laughed. "You don't have to tell us that," she said. "Oh, we know that. But we have hit on something, haven't we?"

I glanced sideways at the women. They looked so sly, so smug. They had their chins up and their hands folded in just the same way. It seemed to me that I could feel the years between them. The struggles and the hopes, the ins and outs of business, of children, of husbands. The countless secrets that had built up between them. Really, they were no different than me and my mother. They were on one side, and we were on the other. We weren't even friends.

"So," I said. "My mother says we're waiting for trumpets."

"We have the trumpets," Maud said. "That isn't the delay." They looked back and forth among each other. "I'm not sure if you're aware of this, but your mother has demanded a larger cut of the profits."

"What?" I asked.

"It surprises you? I can see that it does. The way she sees it, you two have done most of the work. She's demanding 40 percent for you and 40 percent for her. That leaves just

20 percent for the three of us, to split. I'm sure you can see how unfair this is."

"Are you sure you understood her right?" I asked.

"Yes," they said in unison. For a minute no one spoke. The three of them eyed me so suspiciously, so angrily, that I became afraid. The church was empty. There were three of them and only one of me. A few uneasy seconds passed, then Maud spoke.

"She was clear about it," she said.

"Very clear," said Willow. "And from a friend, that hurts."

"She's had a change of character," Rose said. "And we liked her so well, all of us did."

"It's unexpected," Maud said.

"It is," I said, but really, it wasn't. Not completely. She'd tried, even in the beginning, to exclude them, and I'd noticed the changes in her, too. She'd always wanted things in a strong way, but lately it had gotten worse. She shopped more and returned more things. She'd taken to walking around the hotel in the evenings, checking out the other bungalows and jotting notes on a pad. Just the other night, I'd overheard her tell Joan we should move into the Presidential or the Grand Deluxe Suite.

"Everyone in this room is just as greedy," I said. "I don't feel like I can trust any one of you."

They looked back and forth at each other again, but laughed this time.

"We're not asking you to trust us," said Maud.

"We don't even trust each other," said Willow.

"Not where money's concerned," Rose said.

"The thing we want from you," Maud said, "is for you to tell your mother this: We could really use this money.

I could. The church could. I don't know how much your mother's told you about it, but the church is struggling right now. Ever since that stupid faith healing."

"People still believe," Maud went on. "You can't shake the faith of a true believer, but they've slowed their donations. Some of them have changed churches. Because of it, I'm having trouble making rent on the building. What it comes down to is this: Your mother told us the police are looking for her. If the séance doesn't go the way we want it to, we are going to turn her in."

I let that sink in for a minute. "I should go," I said. "My mother is probably looking for me."

"Of course she is," Maud said, patting my knee with her hand. "Now, we don't want to scare you, Lindsey. I hope we haven't scared you. We're still your friends. We just thought you should be, well, aware of some things. Maybe there's something you can do about it."

"Do you want me to come with you?" Rose asked. "If you want me to, I will. A girl your age shouldn't be going around the city like this, taking cabs. Why don't you let me come?"

"I'll be fine," I said. It seemed like the least of my worries. She told them about Oregon. That was all I could think about. We promised each other we wouldn't tell anyone, but she'd told them.

Maud nodded. "About the séance, tell your mother she can pick the night. We'll arrange our schedules to accommodate it."

"We're team players," Willow said. "We'll work with her schedule."

"We do what we can," said Rose.

Maud took some money out of the collection plate beside her and handed it to me. "For your cab fare," she said. "Oh, and one more thing, if the police approach you about the church again . . ."

"The police haven't approached me about the church."

She looked confused. "Your mother said they came by your old apartment a while back, when you were at the hotel."

"That was because of the church?" Why had she let me believe it was because they'd finally caught up with her?

"Yes," Maud said. "If anyone else asks you, you don't know a thing about the church. You weren't here."

"Okay," I said.

She thrust the collection plate money at me, again, and I put it in my pocket. I took off down the aisle so fast I almost collided with an elderly man with a cane.

"I'm sorry," I said.

"He's fine," the woman beside him said. "He doesn't talk, but he's fine. You didn't even hit him."

He pulled a ladies brooch out of his pocket and tried to push it into my hands, but I stepped back.

"I don't work here," I said. "I'm not a medium."

His face deflated, like I'd stolen his one last hope.

"She's not a medium," the woman shouted in his ear.

He nodded, and they continued walking up together, him leaning on her as well as his cane. When they reached the center of the aisle, his knees buckled and he collapsed to the ground.

I went to help him up, but when Maud and Rose walked over, I left him to them, to the wolves, and hurried to the door. My stomach didn't feel right. I didn't think I could get out of there quickly enough. When I came to the front foyer, the air thickened. The scent of flowers and sweet candles shot down around me in a puff of perfume, and a higher, even stranger version of the song on the piano in the other room piped out of a vent on the floor. In the mirror on the side wall, I caught a glimpse of my own eyes, wide and too bright, in front of what looked like the shadow of Willow or Rose, laughing on the other side of the two-way glass.

I held the door shut behind me when I left. I don't know what I thought I could keep in or out, but I felt like I had to rest for a second and catch my breath. I watched a car move down the street. Someone honked, and a woman called her dog. Ordinary enough sounds, and they comforted me. I tried to think of other things. Calling a cab. Returning to the bungalow. What I would say to my mother. But when I closed my eyes, I saw that man again—the persistent way he'd walked, the tortured tilt of his head. The way he'd seemed hopeful for no reason at all. I shook my head, but his face wouldn't go away.

I hailed the next cab I saw, climbed in, and shut the door. I recognized the driver as the man who'd dropped me off a few minutes earlier. He hadn't left me after all, just circled back. I put my hand on the window, just to feel it there, steady, as the street passed by. I closed my eyes and leaned back in the seat, until the darkness behind my eyes evened the darkness outside. The wind made a sound like a lullaby through the window, and I thought about my mother. Why did she tell them about Oregon? And why on Earth had she lied about the police?

# TWENTY-SIX

When I got back to the hotel, my mother was lying in bed in her nightgown, laughing along with the TV.

"Good meeting?" she asked. She patted the bed to tell me that I should sit down, but I shook my head. The light from the television flickered across her face, turning her teeth blue.

"No," I said.

"The problem with those women is that they have no sense of loyalty. We're a team. It makes us different."

I wanted to believe it. I waited until she looked up from the TV, then I said, "Why did you tell them what happened in Oregon?"

She looked surprised. "I don't know. . . . I guess it slipped."

The quiet way she said it made me think of something I hadn't before. She was not a trusting person. It just wasn't like her to make a careless mistake that could open her up to blackmail in that way. When I added in the fact that the police hadn't actually been looking for her when they'd showed up at the apartment, another possibility occurred to me: What if the police weren't really after us? What if she'd made it all up?

"Were we even on the run when we left Oregon?" I asked.

"I don't understand what you're asking," she said. She picked up the remote and started flipping through the channels, but I put my hand over it to stop her.

"The truth," I said.

She sighed. "If you mean, were the police after me when we left, then no. The police were not after me."

"So we left and changed our names for nothing?" My voice was higher now, almost hysterical in pitch, but I didn't care. I wasn't worried anymore that Joan might come home suddenly or that anyone walking by outside might hear. "You let me worry about it all this time?"

She walked over to me and tried to put her hand on my shoulder, but I stopped her. I was still trying to fig-ure it all out. She must have told the South Node Ladies what she'd told me. They must have all had a laugh at my expense. Then, at the church, Maud must have remem-bered the story and decided it would be a good thing to use against me, knowing all along that my mother couldn't admit it wasn't true.

"It wasn't like that, Lindsey."

I glared at her. "What was it like, then? Tell me."

"The way I see it, we *were* on the run. We were running away from being nobodies."

I wanted to shake her. I wanted to knock her to the floor.

"Lindsey," she said in her soft voice, the one that can usually pull me in. "Maybe you think that garage and that small town were big enough for you, but one day you'll thank me. You'll be glad we aren't back there anymore, pretending our lives aren't terrible."

I took a step back, as stunned as if she'd just struck me. I'd never thought our lives were terrible. She'd acted happy, most of the time. Dissatisfied, yes, but happy in a chirpy, crazy bird way. Somehow, her saying our whole lives had been terrible hurt just as much as the lies.

"You don't realize it right now," she said. "But everything I've done in my whole life has been for you. Not for me."

"And I hate you, anyway."

I'd never said anything like that to her before. My voice had an edge to it that surprised me.

She sighed. "Just watch for the switch, Lindsey. It's all you have to do."

"What switch?" I had no idea what she was talking about.

"Later, when you calm down, I'll explain it to you."

That night, just before I went to bed, she came into the living room and sat down on the floor beside the couch.

"Are you calm enough to hear the plan now?" she asked.

"Probably not," I said. "Try me."

In truth, my mind was spinning. Thoughts of Paco and Scott and the scholarships and Joan and her widow money were going around and around, one on the tail of the other like a group of sad dogs I'd disappointed. It's terrible to let people down. It's the worst thing in the world, but it didn't seem to bother my mother.

"Okay," she whispered. "At the séance, when Joan gives us the money, I'll switch it with phony magic store money. Then I'll pass the real money to you. You'll get a prearranged phone call and leave. When you're gone, I'll break the circle. I'll tell Joan we've faked the séance. I'll say that while I am a very good medium, I can't do a physical séance. I'll convince her she talked me into it, but my conscience won't let me continue, and I'll give her the fake money back."

"But I'll have the real money," I said, putting it all together. "And I'll be long gone." It seemed to me that it just might work.

"Right. That's the beauty of it. She won't know we've taken anything, not yet, anyway. And the South Node Ladies won't either. They won't follow us or try to get anything back because they won't know we've got it. I figure we'll have two or three hours after the séance to get to Mexico."

She waited for me to say something. When I didn't, she said, "Understand?"

I did understand, but not like she meant. The big thing I understood—the thing I was most sure of—was that I wasn't going to do any of it. I would watch for the switch, just like she said. But after I saw it, I would switch the money back.

A raw smelling wind blew in through the window, and I looked out at the dark courtyard. I felt my shoulders move back, a loosening along my spine as if I were about to split in two and spin out into the sky. I didn't have to look up to know what type of moon I would see: a full moon on the first of April is, almost always, a Betrayer's Moon.

# TWENTY-SEVEN

I took a photograph on the first day of the last week I spent at the Beverly Hills Hotel. My mother was in it, in her leopard print bathing suit, her hot pink flip-flops, and Joan's huge tortoise shell shades. She had the hotel towel wrapped around her waist like a skirt. Joan was beside her, off to the right, wearing a terrycloth cover up and holding the rabbit. Houdini was to be married the next day, and Joan had dressed him up as a groom, in a pink polka-dotted tuxedo and a flowered top hat. In Joan's circles, people often threw elaborate wedding ceremonies for pets, elegant affairs complete with costumes and vows and monogrammed collars, and Joan had, just that week, after a very long, painful search, located a suitable bride for Houdini, a Black Dutch Dwarf named Sue. When Joan held up Houdini, bathed and combed and stuffed like a sausage into his new pink suit, we all stopped what we were doing and laughed. We had all that treachery between us now. All the lies between my mother and me, and all of the bad intentions between the two of us and Joan, but for a second or two, it all disappeared. For the short space of that laugh, we were just ourselves. Friends.

I picked up the camera to capture the moment, but before I could press the button, the rabbit moved. He'd figured it out, I suppose. He'd realized that the costume Joan had put him in wasn't suitable to his breed of animal, and he wanted no part of it. He twisted so suddenly in Joan's arms that she dropped him. The camera caught him like that, in mid-flight. With Joan's arms outstretched behind him, blurred with sun and motion, he looked like a bird, released. He looked like an offering, like the dove of peace.

The wedding ceremony took place two days later, in the Crystal Garden pagoda, at the center of an explosion of flowers. Although nervous beforehand, at the service itself, Houdini appeared pleased. He sat very still through the reading of his vows, and when it was over he hopped after his bride in an interested way. He consummated his marriage in a flower bush before the guests had even gone home.

"I wouldn't have thought he had it in him," Joan said. "He's such an old little rascal. But of course, he saved himself for her."

My mother cried at the wedding. She soaked two Kleenexes and sneezed into several more. Her makeup smeared in streaks on her cheeks. "There is nothing in this world that gets to me like true love," she said.

"Well, it worked out for somebody." Joan repositioned her yellow hat. "And if anyone deserves it, it's Houdini. Stop crying, Debbie. You're such a silly sap."

My mother set her head down on Joan's shoulder, and both of them laughed. But as soon as Joan walked away, the mood changed.

"It's possible there could be a scene at the séance," my mother said. "I hope not. I think I can smooth things over, but I should mention it as a possibility."

"Okay," I said.

"I'm going to bring my smoke bomb. If something goes wrong, say, someone calls the police or someone gets violent, I'll set it off. The smoke is your signal. If you see smoke, run to the window and climb down."

"That's great," I said. "You bring your smoke bomb. Your smoke bomb will make everything okay."

She stepped back, and the sun fell on her face, and I thought, *She knows*. She saw the Betrayer's moon, and she's figured out what I plan to do. I looked past her, at Joan, scrambling through the brush after the rabbit, her high-heeled shoes in one hand and a very tiny tuxedo in the other. Something about the empty, lost way the suit flapped in the wind made the whole world seem to deflate.

"Two more days," I said.

"That's right," my mother said carefully. "Only two more."

A cloud passed over the sun, and the air turned ash gray. My mother coughed. A man pushing a cart of towels came up behind us, whistling, rattling the pavement like an oncoming train.

When I was nine, maybe ten years old, my friends and I used to play a game we called "hop off" on the tracks that ran along the ravine behind my house. The way we played it was this: we'd wait until we felt the rumble of an oncoming train, then we'd hop off. It was the wind we craved. The racket. The chance to dance with death and win, but now, I thought, what if, at the last second, we simply froze? What if we hadn't been able to move?

"Did you know that the South Node Ladies signed me up for the crystal of the month club?" my mother said. "Just so I would have to mail piles of rocks back?"

"How do you know they did it?" I asked.

"Who else would?"

She said something else, something about how they'd stolen a table she'd reserved at an upcoming psychic fair in Venice Beach, but I wasn't really listening. I looked up at the silvery undersides of the leaves and watched them move in the breeze. I thought again about Oregon: me on the tracks in my striped winter hat. I remembered wind. Bright metal. The bitter taste of grass, and the hard, unmovable way the Earth can feel if you slam up against it. My pounding heart, and the spinning winter sky.

The night before the séance, I called Paco to ask him to call me on my cell phone at the appointed time.

"Hi," I said.

"Oh, hey," he said. His voice was cheerful, not angry. I thought he sounded happy to hear from me, but then he said, "I'm seeing someone."

"It's okay," I said. "I'm not trying to get back together. I just wanted to ask you a favor. I need to interrupt something. Can you call me at 12:44 tomorrow night? Just let my phone ring."

"Okay," he said. "Paper or plastic?"

A buzzing sound distorted his voice, and I could hear the mumble of a radio beneath that. Supermarket Muzak, and the voices of people in line.

"Are you going to call me back after I call you?" he asked.

"I thought you were seeing someone else."

He paused. "I'm not seeing anyone else."

"That's good," I said. "I mean for you."

After we said goodbye, I stood there in the hallway for a long time. It's easy to smash and end and ruin things. It's so much harder to make them right.

# TWENTY-EIGHT

When I walked into the bungalow for the séance, the women were seated in a circle at the table. I took my rehearsed place across from Joan and next to my mother.

"We are all here now," my mother said. Her eyes traveled the room, resting on each woman in turn. "We can begin. If you would, Joan, please place your donation at the center of the table."

Joan pulled a thick wad of cash out of her purse and placed it on the table. The bills were crisp, brand new. In the wavering light from the single candle, I could just make out a hundred at the top.

My mother leaned forward and snatched up the money. She wrapped a gray prayer cloth around it, and Rose lit more candles. Our shadows jumped to the wall, and the air of the bungalow thickened until it smelled almost exactly like the narthex of the Gone But Not Forgotten Church.

"Thank you," my mother said. "Now, I have to warn you, at certain times during the séance, something I say may seem silly or not quite right. You might be nervous, but please don't laugh. There's something about laughter that doesn't transmit right and annoys and offends our spirit friends. Also, please don't touch me if I go into a trance. Shock can jolt me too quickly back into my body. If you see a trumpet fly in the air and tip toward you, you can cup your hands to receive an apport, but try not to touch the trumpet itself."

I almost laughed. I was nervous, I suppose, and she'd made me want to by telling me not to. I had to bite my lip to keep my face straight. When I regained my composure, I put my hands on the table and touched fingers with the people on either side of me, my mother and Willow.

We said a short prayer and sang a hymn and my mother asked for the protection of the white light. Some fog went up. Just our dry ice, but it felt like the breath of the dead.

"My gatekeeper is here," my mother whispered. She had explained before that everyone has five major spirit guides, one of which acts as a gatekeeper. This spirit, who is sometimes called a joy guide, controls the vibration of the room and works as a mediator between the physical and spiritual worlds. My mother's gatekeeper went by the name of Martha Bigsby.

The white curtain rustled in the window, and the rehearsed, tape-recorded laugh started. The sudden, dizzy scent of flowers wafted in, followed by the cold, chlorine breath of the pool.

Martha Bigsby's laugh was Rose's cue. She stood up on a chair to turn on the red light. It took my eyes a second to adjust. In the church, the red light had made the sides and the corners of things glow in a sinister way, but here, in the bungalow, it seemed almost peaceful. Like firelight, but redder, and without the flicker. As I reached down beneath the tablecloth to bring up my trumpet, I felt strangely calm. I lifted it very slowly, taking care not to drop it or to bump the table. Black paint disappears in red light, so the handle looked invisible. I might have believed it was floating, myself, if I hadn't felt cold, smooth metal in my hands. I lifted the shiny, visible head of the trumpet up to the spot just above the center of the table, and circled it around three times. Willow fumbled a bit with her own trumpet. She did something that made a sound like a coin dropping in the dark, but when she said, "I am the one who in life you called Saul," it was all right.

The trumpet circled above Joan, and someone (it must have been my mother) threw something on the table.

"It's for you, Joan," my mother said, "an apport."

An apport is a gift from the spirit world. In this case, a gold bracelet. We bought it at Macy's to replace one Joan had lost at the hotel, but we must not have gotten it exactly right because Joan looked confused when she picked it up. She set it back down on the table like she didn't recognize it at all, and cupped her hands beneath the trumpet for another gift.

"There is nothing else in the trumpet," my mother said in a spooky voice.

She began to shake all over. She shut her eyes and went completely still, like the fortune-teller doll in arcades, the one that comes suddenly to life when you give her a quarter. Then she jerked her head violently and coughed phony ectoplasm up onto the table. I was more than a little embarrassed for her, watching it, but Joan just looked surprised. My mother leaned forward, still coughing, and I felt her pass the money to me underneath the table. Her fingernails scraped my palm lightly as she pushed the wool-wrapped package into my hands.

The switch. I ran my fingers over the bundle. It seemed light. I placed it in my lap, between my knees, and looked at the table, at what was now the cloth-wrapped magic store money.

"He's here," my mother croaked out, in a large, man-like version of her own voice, and Maud appeared in the hallway, cloaked in a saran-wrap ensemble. She flapped around the dining room table and floated into the living room where she did a very large loop around the couch. In the red light, she looked transparent. Her black suit disappeared much as the trumpet handle had, and her body in the saran wrap seemed to float of its own accord. The noise of crinkling bubble-soaked plastic was distinguishable, just below the music we'd rigged to disguise it.

It was time. I felt my breath catch, but my hand, reaching for the money, was surprisingly steady. I didn't think of my mother or the chaos I knew would surely erupt later. I thought only of Joan. I watched her nodding profile as I wrapped the money in the prayer cloth underneath the table. When she turned to me, finally, I managed to smile. The red light flickered. For a second, everything seemed very clear to me, as if a camera flash had gone off and the world was outlined briefly in black and white.

I looked around the table. Rose was moving her head, slowly, to the odd, underwater beat of Maud's dance. Willow was trying to pretend to look surprised. My mother just smiled, as if nothing about this night were out of the ordinary at all. Joan sat very still, with her hands in her lap, and a puzzled, slightly hopeful expression on her face.

When Maud turned the corner into the other room, leaving a trail like a slug, Paco called.

"I have a call," I said. "I have to leave."

"Go ahead, Lindsey," my mother said. She shooed me with her hand, but I stayed in my seat.

"I have something to tell you, Joan," I said.

"You should leave," my mother said. "You're interrupting."

"In a second," I said. I looked down at the money on the table, the real money. I didn't even want it. The room went silent, and the air gathered around me.

"I lied to you, Joan," I said. "We all did. We told you a lot of lies." It was a relief to say it. I felt as light as a balloon.

A buzzing noise started, from off to the left, and the red lights burned brighter. I could just make out the faint rustling sound of Maud in the next room, sliding out of her bubble-coated, saran-wrap robe.

My mother stood and took a step back from the table. "Lindsey's right," she said. "We can't do this séance. I'm sorry, Joan." She pushed what she thought was the phony money in front of Joan.

"Sit down, Debbie," Willow said.

"You say you can't do it," Rose said, "but we all saw Saul. Didn't we, girls? Just a second ago. You brought him up, Debbie."

"It wasn't real," I said.

It might have been an effect of the red light, but everything began to move in slow motion. Willow stuffed her trumpet under her jacket, and my mother put her hand on her chair. Rose wiped a bit of phony ectoplasm off her sleeve.

"I'll do the talking, Lindsey," my mother said.

"What I saw," Rose said, "was a spectacular spirit manifestation and the church will verify it."

Joan looked down at her hands and twisted her wedding ring with her finger. "Let me understand this. You're saying that you're frauds? All of you?"

Rose gasped. "No!"

"Certainly not," Willow said. She stood, setting her glasses down on the table. Without them, her eyes looked small and extremely alarmed. "Don't include us in that group."

"We're all frauds," I said. I switched the light on and held up my trumpet. "It's got a black handle, see. It disappears in red light. And Willow talks through another one."

Willow looked away. With the light on, I could see the black powder she had used to coat her arms. She had a dot on her nose where she must have rubbed it.

"I wouldn't say I'm a fraud," my mother said, carefully, "but I can't perform a physical séance."

"What does that mean?" Joan asked me.

"I don't understand it either," I said. "But I'll tell you another thing."

"That's enough, Lindsey," my mother said, but I wasn't about to stop.

"We looked you up online," I said. "We looked up your husband, too."

"You need to shut up, Lindsey," Willow said. She leaned against the table and sunk her fingernails into my hand. I managed to pull my arm away, but the marks she left felt hot, as if she'd just burned me.

A rustling sound started, and Maud appeared in the room. She'd taken her costume off, but she still had a bit of the phony ectoplasm on her shirt. Her hair stood up on one side, and her left foot dragged a piece of saran wrap.

She must have heard everything, back in the room, but she managed, somehow, to look surprised. Her lips puckered in an indignant way.

"Debbie and Lindsey should leave the séance," she said. "I'm here now. We have enough people to continue." She smiled as if she were stating who might stay for tea.

Joan turned her head. "Shut up," she snapped.

My mother opened her mouth to say something, but before she could, Maud shoved her. My mother teetered and fell to the ground, and Maud stepped forward and kicked her face. I leapt out of my chair and threw myself on top of Maud. I might have been able to stop her, but Willow jumped on my back. She hung from my neck, pulling at my hair, while I swung her little body again and again around the room.

"Now, this," Joan said, "is ridiculous." She picked up the phone. "I'm calling the police."

At the word *police*, a cloud of smoke rose up. It lasted only a few short seconds, and when it faded, my mother was gone. The rest of us turned to face each other. No one but me knew exactly what had happened or whose trick it had been.

# TWENTY-NINE

After my mother disappeared, I walked out the door and hailed a cab to Santa Monica. No one stopped me. I just left.

The pier was eerily quiet. Most of the tourists had left. Only a few of the heavier drinkers remained, sprawled face down on benches or stumbling through the salty air. A group of fishermen in bright, feathered hats stood along one side of the pier. I watched them throw their arms back and swing their poles forward, until their hooks disappeared into the sky. It seemed possible to me that they might catch a star. I would have liked to watch them some more, but I knew if I did, I would lose my nerve. I might never be able to face my mother.

I took a deep breath to steady myself. Then I stepped over a paper cup and a box of spilled french fries and started across the pier. I found my mother sitting on the last bench, facing the sea with her knees drawn up, tucked into the front of her enormous windbreaker jacket. Huddled down like that, she could have been just about anyone.

"Did anyone follow you?" she asked. Her voice was raw in the wind.

"I don't think so," I said.

"Good," she said. "Well, it's done. We did it."

It was what she used to say in Oregon, at Girl Scout cookie time, when we went out to sell the cookies. I had a sudden memory of us, knocking on various doors in the rain, carrying our cookie order forms. We'd really enjoyed selling those cookies. We jumped around the kitchen when the boxes arrived, and we grinned like Christmas morning as we handed them out. The other mothers would sit in their vans or stand a few feet back on the street, but she always walked beside me, pushing my pile of cookies in her stolen shopping cart. It always seemed like we had a much better time than anyone else.

She stood up on the dock, and her skinny legs jutted out like sticks beneath her wind-filled jacket. She looked so joyful, like a giant, flapping white bird, that for a second, I didn't think I could tell her. I didn't think I could bear to watch her come crashing down.

"I've always wanted to live by the sea," she said. "We'll get a little house with orange tiles on the roof. Maybe something on a hill. Maybe Puerto Vallarta. What do you think?"

"I don't know," I said. The thing was, I could see that place by the sea. I looked away from her, out at the ocean, vast and silvery gray. It was raining lightly. It didn't make much of a difference to us standing there, but lightening moved across the sea. For a second, the sky was bright and everything was visible, the boats and buoys and low-flying birds, but then the overwhelming blackness moved in again.

"Well, it doesn't have to have an orange roof," she said. "You never liked orange. I'll tell you what, you pick the roof."

"I have something to tell you," I said.

She turned to face me. Up close, she looked tired, older than she had ever looked, and I could tell, even in this light, that a dark, blue-black spot had formed beneath her left eye in the place where Maud had kicked her. I wished I could hug her. I wished I was a little girl again, that the giant thing I had done when I'd switched the money hadn't happened yet, and I could wrap my arms around her neck and ask her to take me home.

I took a deep breath. "I don't have the money," I said.

"I know," she said.

"You know?"

She nodded. "I'm your mother. I knew."

She laughed, and the wind snatched the sound away. "I knew you would switch it, so I waited until the end. Then I switched it back." She motioned to her suitcase. "It's in here."

"What?" I picked up the suitcase, but before I could open it to check, two police cars appeared at the end of the dock. They parked at a diagonal, blue lights flashing, and four men in uniform got out. A car door slammed, followed by the sound of heavy steps on wood. I scanned the dark dock for moving shapes.

"It's the police," I said, and I felt my entire body freeze. I could no longer feel my feet or hear my heart.

"It'll be all right," my mother said. Her voice seemed to come out of nowhere, out of another time. I had a vision of the hallway of the shotgun house, her head popping up into the rectangle of light in the doorway to chase away a bad dream. The officers were getting closer. They were four growing shadows at the far end of the pier.

"Just give me the suitcase," she said, "and it'll be all right."

"I'm a minor," I said. "They'll go easier on me."

She pried the suitcase out of my fingers just before the beam of light hit us.

# THIRTY

There aren't that many people who will take a suitcase full of thousands of dollars out of your hands and face the police holding it. My mother is one of those few. I thought about this at the police station, in the bright hallway, on the small blue plastic chair where they told me to wait.

I sat there for a long time, maybe all night. I didn't sleep, although at one point, the edges of things blurred and went black, and I thought I saw my mother materialize at the door. They'd separated us hours ago, handcuffed her, and taken her away.

*What have I done?* I asked her apparition, but it just shimmered slightly and disappeared.

Eventually, a woman showed up in the hallway and motioned to me to follow her. Her face was pale and tired. Was it possible it was still night? She led me to a room, and we both sat down. Then she spread some papers out on a table. She leaned back in her chair and stretched her left arm up, like the wing of a bird, and rotated it at the shoulder. I couldn't help but feel sorry for her. It had to be a hard job, questioning juveniles. I could see how it might make a person think they had acquired a broken wing.

"Are you finished crying now?" she asked.

I nodded. I thought so.

"Good," she said. "Because I have a few questions for you."

"I'd like to have a lawyer present for that," I said in a firm voice. One thing I'd noticed, lately, was that the way you talk to people matters more than what you say. The voice that came out of my mouth at first was mixed. It started off sounding a lot like my mother, but in the end it was mine.

"We'll get to that if we need to," she said. "But first, let me ask you this. Do you think you can tell me why your mother was carrying a suitcase of fake money?"

I was about to insist on the lawyer again, but then I replayed her question in my head. "She was carrying fake money?" I asked.

She looked at me sideways. "Come on now. Surely you knew."

"I did not know she was carrying fake money," I said truthfully. She'd said on the pier it was real, that she'd switched it.

She tapped her pencil on the table, and I looked at my hands. The cut from my mother's fingernail when she'd grabbed the suitcase from me was still there, bleeding slighting in a jagged red line.

"We've located the stolen money," she said. "Would you like to know where?"

"Please," I said.

"We apprehended three women outside the hotel carrying it. I'm guessing you know who the women are?"

I did, but I pretended to look confused.

"We've talked to Joan Fields. She's not pressing charges against you or your mother."

I stopped separating the tissue she'd thrown at me into tiny pieces. "What about the South Node . . . the others."

She raised her eyebrows. "Is it important?"

"I guess not," I said.

All of us, then, had switched the money. I should have planned for that.

"You can meet your mother outside," she said. "You're both free to go."

# THIRTY-ONE

After the police let us go, we returned to the Sepulveda complex and moved back in. The landlord had made some improvements. He'd patched the roof, and painted the walls, and replaced the carpet with a cheap yellow laminate throughout. I could still smell cat, but only around the curtains and only in certain spots.

The drawback to all of the updates was that our rent had gone up. My mother spent the afternoon on the phone, fighting with the landlord. In her mind, *he* owed *her* money because she'd paid rent all those months we'd stayed at the hotel. She paced the balcony in her Big Bird bathrobe, waving the phone at any neighbors who peeked out, while I sat slumped beside her on the plastic chair, staring glumly across the courtyard at Paco's apartment. I traced the shape of the moonstone necklace he gave me for Christmas into my notebook and wrote:

*Mooonstone. It's said to have the power to reuinite lovers. Why doesn't it work?*

I looked over at the window. I could leave the necklace on the sill tonight to charge in the moon, but the stairs were too close. Anyone walking by could take it, and I would miss it too much. I held it up and watched the light dart across it. At a certain angle, I thought I could see the crescent moon.

When evening came, we went inside. We opened all the windows and let the highway wind blow in. My mother turned on the TV to drown out the noise. The news, again. A car chase. Someone was rushing to Mexico, southbound on the 405 with an illegal substance in his car. I walked over to the window, waited a few minutes, and watched it all pass by. The car came first, small and black and extraordinarily fast, just a blur of darkness against the darker night, followed by sirens and rolling blue lights. Next, the helicopter arrived. It hovered a moment, making a chopping sound, before it lifted up, shaking the apartment as it went by. The little black car would never make it, but I wished him luck. I wondered if there might be some minor angel, assigned to thieves like us.

How can I describe the last two months of my senior year? It was a formality, a thing to trudge through. I went to all of my classes. I pretended to care, and when the lunch bell rang, I ate with Emily. I tried not to look at Paco, sitting across the courtyard with Scott, but sometimes I did, out of the corner of my eye. The ghosts of the living can haunt you. They are every bit as persistent as the dead.

"You should talk to him," Emily said.

"It wouldn't do any good," I said.

She nodded. I guess she agreed. "Hey, did you hear about the scholarships?"

"No," I said. "What?"

"They're going to announce it next period, but everyone already knows."

"They do?" I asked. I didn't talk to that many people anymore. It didn't surprise me I was behind on the news.

"They aren't taking away the scholarships after all. The church came up with the money to finish everyone out."

"They did?" It surprised me, but really, it shouldn't have. Church people like to give money; it had been the basis of our scam.

It probably had to do with the good news, but that afternoon, I finally got up the nerve to knock on Paco's door.

"Hi," I said.

He leaned against the doorframe. "Hey."

"I wanted to say . . ." I looked over at the pool, at the tarp blowing up. "I'm sorry. For, you know, everything."

I snuck a look at him. He appeared to be thinking it over. He was still leaning against the door, but now he had his thumbs in his pockets. After a while he said, "Okay."

"Okay?"

He laughed. "That's what I said. Okay."

I can't tell you how good it felt to be forgiven. My relief felt huge, as wide as the sky.

"So we're friends now," I said carefully.

He nodded.

I felt encouraged enough by this to ask for more. "I mean, I know you wouldn't take me back or anything. . . ."

He laughed. "I might."

We sat down on the steps, in our usual spot, and faced the courtyard. After a while, he took my hand.

"I heard about the scholarships," I said.

He nodded.

"Maybe they'll get money for the playground, too," I said.

"Nah. We had a meeting about that yesterday. They're calling it off."

I thought about the playground and the kids who wouldn't have it because of me, and then I thought about Joan. I remembered the way she used to walk, slowly, with one ear tipped, as if she were listening for Saul, and the crumpled way she could look, sometimes, in a hotel bathrobe. The way she could sit for hours, looking out the window at pure darkness, tapping her foot. We'd hurt her. I wouldn't, as long as I lived, be able to change or forget about that.

"I'm sorry," I said.

"Yeah, well, you didn't do it." He leaned back on his arms and looked up at the sky. "And we're young, right? We still have time to change the world."

"Yeah?" I believed it could be true. I'd done some things I wished I hadn't, but I guess I still felt hopeful. "I think I might start with the Hippocratic Oath, though. You know, do no harm."

A door opened behind us. A short, round woman with a flushed face and a toddler between her legs stepped out to shake a rug over the balcony rail. I watched the dust flap down to the courtyard. A group of migrating birds— the bright, orange topped, yellow bellied type that visit Los Angeles for a few months each spring—turned from their perch on the lower balcony rail to look at us. I felt something rise inside me when they lifted up.

There was only one person left to apologize to now. I climbed into the car and drove to Malibu. I took the winding roads higher, until the air thinned and the light took on the shimmering quality of new coins in the sun. I wasn't sure I would find the house; the road detoured, and the landmarks I remembered were just not there. But then I saw it. I parked at the bottom of the driveway, in the spot we'd left our car for the grocery swap.

Joan's new house looked much different than her old one. It was wide, rather than tall, and it had a long panel of windows across the front. It had none of the grandness or the stark elegance of the first one, and I thought maybe this was what Joan wanted all along—a home that squatted rather than hovered, that stood with windows flung open, facing the sea. All those nights at the hotel, I never looked carefully at Joan's plans for her house.

I started up the stone path, but before I reached the door, it opened and Joan stepped out. She was wearing a pair of cut-off jean shorts, and she had two lime green gardening gloves in her hand. When she noticed me standing there, she paused.

"Joan," I said. "I'm sorry." I hadn't meant to open the conversation like that. I'd meant to build up to my apology, but that was how it came out. "I wouldn't believe me if I were you, but I mean it."

She put her hand up to shield her eyes from the sun, and I couldn't read her face.

"I wanted to tell you the truth," I said. "So many times."

"I believe you." She was quiet for a few seconds. "I suspected it sometimes."

"You did?"

"I've always been open to the idea that the dead can communicate with us." She looked up at the sky. "I still believe it's possible. But there was something about the way you two went about it that didn't always seem right."

"Yeah," I said. I could see how that would be true. "But you never said anything."

"I didn't."

I thought about what she'd said that night last winter about not wanting to leave the hotel, and suddenly, I understood. She'd liked having us there. She hadn't brought up her doubts because she'd wanted us to stay. I wondered if she was still lonely.

"Are you okay here? Do you like the new house?"

"I do," she said. "It's been a good change for me. A fresh start."

I looked across the lawn, at the tennis court, and thought about how we would never get to play.

"It really is a nice house," I said.

"Thank you," she paused. After a second she said, "I'm going to head around back now. There are some very scraggly rose bushes that require my attention." She put her gardening gloves on and took a step to the left.

"I'm changing," I said. "I'm trying really, really hard."

"You'll be okay, Lindsey." She started to walk away, but then she turned and said, "Just keep your eyes on the sky."

The next week, I arranged to meet with the principal in her office. Graduation was coming up, and I wanted to see my real name on the diploma. I wanted to use it next year when I started at UCSC.

"We can certainly contact the school," she said when I asked her about it. "But to tell you the truth, I don't know what will happen. You got in with the other name."

"I know," I said, "but I still want to do it."

She looked at me for a long moment. "I had a student once who went through something like this—a domestic situation with a dangerous parent. Am I getting close, here, to your situation?"

"No," I said. "My situation is more that my mother made it all up."

She turned her head sideways, and her glasses caught the light.

"There was no bad or good parent," I said to clarify. "Just my mother."

"I see," she said. She leaned back in her chair and pressed her hands together in the shape of a church.

"I don't think I can explain it better than that," I told her, "but I really, really want to go to this school."

"I'll try my best," she said. "I'll see what I can do."

I turned eighteen in June. My mother baked a round chocolate cake with blue and yellow icing, four layers tall. It collapsed in the center as soon as we lit the candles, but it tasted all right. Paco brought his sisters over, and we all ate it on the balcony, under a candy pink sky. The girls danced around the candles and sang "Cumpleaños Feliz" and fought with each other over who should be the one to sit on my lap.

When the cake was gone, Paco hung a piñata and handed his smallest sister a bat. At first, she faltered under the weight of it. She tripped, righted herself, and walked blindly to the steps to swing at the railing. But then she got it right. *Smack*, and the donkey spun. *Smack*, and another sister took a turn. In the end, Paco had to smash it. The little girls squeeled when it burst in the sky.

The day after my birthday, I took a summer job as a waitress. I wouldn't find out the outcome of the principal talking to the school until July, but I started to save up some money of my own, anyway. The restaurant was small, with indoor picnic tables and peanut shells on the ground. I never did come around to liking the peanuts. It was hard to overlook the constant crunching sound they made, and I had to pick them out of the soles of my shoes every night, but otherwise, the restaurant was nice enough. It had its own ebb and flow, its own beat. I liked the customers (a mix of tourists and regulars) who came in. I liked hearing where they were from and guessing where they were going, and I liked the way the waitstaff gathered at a back table at the end of the shift until the manager realized we were all there and shouted at everyone to leave. I liked the easy way that money appeared in piles on the tables. It seemed like a gift to me. All this time, it was so much easier than I ever thought.

Sometimes, after my shift, I'd spread out my tarot cards on the back table. I didn't read for other people, anymore, only for myself. It was just a way to pass the time between shifts, but then, one day, it was different. What I mean is (and I know how crazy this sounds) I began to understand from these cards a fuzzy slip of my own future.

The day I drew the Five of Wands (a card of minor irritations), my computer stopped working, I stubbed my toe, and a stray cat slipped into our apartment and peed on the rug. I wrote it off as coincidence, until later that afternoon, when I turned over the Wheel of Fortune card and became the 115th customer of the day at Ralphs. I won a free recyclable tote bag, a month's worth of coupons, and the opportunity to choose any one free item from my cart. I chose a family pack of chicken wings for $10.11.

The day I turned over the World card, I got a letter from the school. They were going to let me in, pending the transcripts from my real school in Oregon, but the process would cause a delay. I wouldn't be able to start until the second semester. Still, I had my name back. I can't tell you how good it felt just to see it on the outside of that envelope: Lindsey Allen instead of Lindsey Smith.

Even though I wouldn't be able to start school until January, I made plans to move out right away. Emily was renting an apartment with two girls who were starting with her at Santa Monica College in the fall and they all said they didn't mind having me for a few months, as long as I paid rent.

"I thought you would live at home," my mother said when I told her. "At least until you started school."

She walked across the room to the window, and the sun hit her face. Her hair was blond again, the light buttery shade I remembered from my childhood. Seeing it that way made me long for her, somehow, even though she was right there with me in the room.

"People move out when they turn eighteen," I said.

She looked out the window. "I suppose they do."

"It's only a couple miles," I said.

"Oh," she said. "Is that all?"

"That's all," I said.

I looked down at the arm of the couch, at the lines that crisscrossed the nubby fabric, like roads on a map. I knew I was disappointing her. I knew she wouldn't be able to run the psychic business on her own, but I guess it wasn't enough to change my mind. I guess I just saw my shot at a normal life and decided to take it.

I moved into Emily's apartment in August. I would only be staying until December, but it felt like a huge thing. Paco came with me to help unpack. My mother did, too, but just before we stepped into the elevator, she acted like she might change her mind.

"You'll die," she said. "You'll fall down the shaft."

She clung to the railing as we rode it up, and when we got out, she claimed she'd seen a cockroach in the hall, that it had run over her toe.

"Did you see where it went?" Paco asked.

"It didn't go anywhere," I said. "Because it doesn't exist."

He tapped the wall anyway. "It sounds solid. Of course, there could be a million creepy crawlies inside." He smirked like a little boy bringing a little girl something disgusting, like a worm pie.

"I see it," I lied, "there, on your back."

He stopped smiling and jumped.

When we got to the door, Emily was waiting next to her mother. She looked like her, but shorter, and with red bobbed hair.

"I'm Susan," she said to us. "We've lost the key."

"I have one," I said. I opened the door and looked inside. The kitchen was small and I didn't see a balcony, but the carpet in the living room looked new and the walls had fresh paint.

"Go ahead," my mother said. She shooed me forward with her hand. "You two go first."

I walked in and Emily followed. She ran her finger along the front counter. "This place needs some Lysol. Mom!"

Emily's mom whipped out a can of Lysol and sprayed it around, while my mother moved into the kitchen and pretended to help. She opened and closed all the drawers, pushing things around. After a while, she took out an ugly orange potholder she'd brought to give me and hung it up on a nail on the wall. "Here? What do you think?"

"Wherever," I said. I figured I could move it or trash it after she left.

"I always wanted one like this," she said.

"You did?" It always made me sad when she wanted small things. "You keep it." I took it down from the wall and handed it to her.

"But I want you to have it," she said and pressed it back into my hand. I didn't know what to do with it—this orange potholder that she wanted for me, but that I didn't want. It didn't seem right to just stuff it in a drawer, so I hung it back on the hook and left it there.

"It's hard to believe," she sighed, "but my girl is leaving."

"I'm moving out. It's a different thing," I said, because I already knew the truth: It's not possible to ever, completely leave your mother. You can try, as I did, but she will haunt you like a ghost. She will possess your body, your gestures, the movements of your hands. She'll state her opinions about just about everything. She'll inhabit your dreams and your heart and your memories and the faces of your children to come.

"Lindsey," she called from the window. "Come over here. I want to show you something." Her voice had that excited quality to it—the too-high tone it sometimes got that had always reminded me of birds in the spring.

"What is it? I'm doing something." But I walked over anyway. I watched her open the Venetian blind, and looked in the direction that she pointed.

"If you lean out tonight, I think you might be able to see the moon."

"You think so?" I asked.

"I think so."

I leaned out the window and turned my head around until I grew dizzy, until the people on the street swirled below me in a colorful, mixed-up stew. I felt the hot sun on the side of my face. If I stretched, I could almost see a patch of white sky. It was easy enough, anyway, to imagine a good omen moon, to believe that on the right kind of night, I might be able to see one.

# ACKNOWLEDGMENTS

I would like to thank my insightful editor, Nicole Frail, and everyone else at Sky Pony Press, especially Emma Dubin and Erin Seaward-Hate.

I'd also like to thank my extraordinary agent, Regina Brooks, and her helpful team at Serendipity Literary Agency.

Thank you to my writing group: Cathy Cruise, Colleen Kearney Rich, and Ruth Boggs, who have read so many drafts of this book they've probably lost count. Other early readers and advisors who gave invaluable suggestions and support were: Carolyn Parkhurst, Susann Cokal, Urvashi Varma, Cherise Fisher, and Rachel Schwartz.

Thank you to my parents, Joe and Elsie Scimecca, for believing in me, and to my sister, Faith, for providing encouragement along the way.

A special thank you to my daughters, Julia and Natalie, who inspire me every day, and to my husband, Tony, without whose unwavering love and support this book would not have been possible.